Autumn Lady

To: Cortney,

I'm so happy for the day we met. You have been an absolute blessing and dear friend. I hope you enjoy the story of autumn Lady. Happy reading!

Love.

AnneMarie

Autumn Lady

by AnneMarie Dapp

Published by
Torrid Books
An imprint of Whiskey Creek Press LLC
Torridbooks.com

Cover Artist: Kelly Martin
Editor: Dennis Hays
Printed in the United States of America

Print ISBN: **978-1-63596-686-2**

Acknowledgements

I would like to thank my friends and family for their support during the writing of this novel. My husband, Dale, and our children, Eric and Lindsay, were true inspirations.

I am forever grateful for my best friends, Darci and Maria. Your encouragement and feedback was priceless.

Thank you, Steven and David Rockwell, for your belief in your little sister.

I'd also like to give a huge shout-out to Torrid Books and their amazing staff. There were so many wonderful people that helped me along the way. Your names could easily fill an entire book.

Lastly, I want to thank our Heavenly Father for his guidance and strength, during this beautiful journey.

~ AnneMarie Dapp

Dedication

For Grandmom John

BOOK ONE

Chapter 1

Her high heels clicked over the marble floor. A pleated skirt brushed against her long legs. She stopped in front of the black door, hands trembling. Taking a deep breath, she reluctantly turned the cold doorknob. It opened to a well-lit penthouse. An impressive view of downtown San Francisco behind a walnut desk. Floor to ceiling windows revealed a thick fog moving between shimmering skyscrapers. Seagulls floated by like lost souls in the mist. A portly man quickly stood up from his leather chair, hands outstretched, eager to please.

"It's been quite a while, Mary."

"Yes. It's been a long time," she answered numbly. It took some effort to force a smile on her face. She reached out and shook her lawyer's hand. It was soft and plump.

"Please have a seat. Something to drink? A coffee? Soda?"

"That's very kind. No. I'm fine."

"Well, I'm sure you're anxious to get down to business. I imagine you're exhausted after all of the funeral arrangements." He smiled gently.

"I've been trying to take it day by day."

The lawyer pulled out the drawer next to his desk. He opened a large manila folder, pulling his glasses away from his face, examining the paperwork.

"The details regarding the estate are in these documents. I'm sure it's no surprise…your grandmother, Helen, left everything to you."

Mary pushed her dark curls behind her ears. A nervous habit. She let out a deep sigh. *Mom should be in this chair. Not me.* She strained not to give in to the tears welling behind her eyes.

"Mary, did you hear what I said?"

The young woman looked up startled. "I'm sorry. Could you repeat that?"

"Of course. I was just saying that your grandmother made sure to include her housekeeper and gardener in the will. Their salaries have been taken care of for the remainder of their service to the estate. They will be paid monthly from the bank account."

Mary smiled at the news. Joseph and Margaret had been taking care of the home for decades. It was a relief to know they would continue working for her. They were the closest thing to a family she had anymore.

"That's great. I'm thrilled they'll be staying on."

"Very good. I'm glad that works for you."

Over the next couple hours, she signed the seemingly endless copies of paperwork. When she left the office, the young woman was officially a homeowner. This was not how she imagined her life playing out.

She changed out of her pumps, into a pair of tennis shoes from her backpack, and climbed onto her bright green Vespa. After she secured her helmet, she turned on the engine and zipped through the downtown Financial District. The cold air gave her a shock. She made her way down Van Ness Avenue, passing Saint Brigid Cathedral along the way. An old memory surfaced, her grandmother leading her down a long aisle. Shiny Mary Janes squeaked as she walked. She looked up at Father Peter offering Communion. *God bless you, child,* in his thick Irish accent. The elderly priest gently making the sign of the cross over her forehead. The scent of candles was comforting. She gazed upwards in anticipation. Soon they would be going to Sunday Brunch. She'd have a grilled cheese and French fries. That was her favorite. There would be ice cream afterwards. The light turned red as her Vespa eased to a stop. A taxi driver cursed at a bike messenger cutting out in front. The boy peddled by grinning. The light turned green and she made her way down toward Pacific Heights. After finding her turnoff, she took a left and continued her way onto the sidewalk. She shifted to neutral and searched for her keys in her backpack. Finding them, she walked down to the wrought iron gate. Sharp, metal points rose towards the heavens. The lock clicked and the gate opened with a loud groan. She brought her bike through and locked the door behind her. Once inside, the sound of falling water eased her mind. An impressive fountain stood at the center of the lush lawn. Two porcelain angels embraced as water rolled down their snowy wings. Pansies were planted at the base. The purple and orange petals matched the rich paint of the old Victorian. She walked the bike down the cobblestones, following the curve of the manicured lawn. The ancient estate waited. Rose bushes lined the walkway. Shaded behind a large pink tree rose, an elderly man was busy pruning. He looked up for a moment from his work as a smile spread over his wrinkled face.

"Mary…"

She smiled at the gardener. "Joseph, I hope you're not working too hard."

"This work is good for an old man like me. Keeps me out of trouble, the misses says." His kind eyes shone through the fog.

Mary smiled.

She walked toward the old home lost in thought, eventually finding herself at the bottom steps. Two regal lions rested on each side of the banister. The old Victorian had always left her breathless. The estate had been built in the 1870s. Her great-grandfather had seen to every detail of the spectacular home— a wedding present to his wife, Great Grandmother Mara. Stained glass windows framed the double doors. The glass was flecked with a mixture of deep orange, purple, and yellow. Looking through the oval windows offered a colorful view of the parlor. A figure eclipsed the glass and made her flinch. The large bronze doors opened. The smell of cinnamon and warm baked bread greeted her. An elderly woman beamed as she held out her plump arms.

"Mary, dear girl, what a pleasure. Come in." The matronly woman wrapped her arms around her like a soft blanket. The scent of rose petals and fresh linen.

"Margaret, I'm so happy you're staying on. I couldn't imagine this place without you."

"Ah, Mary. We wouldn't dream of being anywhere else. Now, my poor dear, you look exhausted. Why don't yah come in an' have a cup of tea and some scones. You look thin as a bean pole, my poor child."

Mary smiled at the housekeeper. She accepted her offer happily. Her eyes searched the grand room. The home never failed to fill her with a sense of awe. Two dramatic staircases of polished mahogany spiraled on each side of the parlor, leading to the second story. The upstairs featured richly decorated bedrooms, sitting areas, and baths. Each room contained a collection of vintage antiques acquired over many decades. On sunny days, the stained glass windows illuminated the parlor, transforming the room into a colorful lightshow. The back wall displayed a large oil painting. The artwork had been completed the year the house was built, 1873. The sun's rays managed to penetrate the fog belt outside the windows. A colorful beam of light caressed the face of the portrait subject.

A young woman stood beneath the flowing branches of an old oak tree—its leaves reflecting the vibrant autumn colors of the stained glass. Strawberry blonde curls flowed from beneath a cheery blue bonnet, her hair the color of smoking cinders. Flecks of gold appeared to have been mixed into the paint. The brushstrokes reminded Mary of paintings created by Impressionist artists in the 19th century. The composition seemed to be moving with an electrical rhythm, broken up by dabs of color; but you could still make out the minute details, like the long lashes framing soft blue eyes. A rosy blush shone on her fair skin. Delicate pursed lips lifted slightly in the corners as if she found the moment amusing. A blue satin gown was cinched tightly around the tiny waist and flowed softly against the autumn colored leaves. Her gloved hands held the reins of the petite sorrel mare standing at her side. The horse's crimson mane shone brilliantly in the afternoon light as she eyed her mistress with affection.

Mary studied the image with fascination. Her musings were suddenly interrupted by the sound of Margaret's voice calling her from the kitchen. "The tea's ready if you'd like some, dear."

She moved away from the portrait, toward the kitchen. Not much had changed since she was a child. The room was still the same collection of old teakettles, cups and vintage wallpaper. An old-fashioned stove was in the corner. The antique oak table was set for two. A crystal vase filled with fresh roses rested on a flowered tablecloth.

Fog moved past the windows, darkening the room. Margaret poured tea into Mary's cup. Little shamrocks decorated the fine china. Margaret placed a blueberry scone on a matching pastry plate.

This warm kitchen brought back so many memories. She recalled her grandmother busy stirring a cocoa while sugar cookies baked in the oven. The scent of cinnamon hung in the air. Rain pattered gently against the window in a room which was always a sanctuary.

"Well now, child, it's so good to have you back. It's been quite lonesome without your grandmother in the house. We miss her so. I know she's watching after you from heaven, just like your dear mother."

Mary looked up, her large brown eyes glistening with tears. "Thank you, Margaret. Yes, I definitely feel close to them here. I'll be bringing my things at the end of the week, but I brought an overnight bag with me today. I just don't have the energy to go back to my apartment tonight."

"Well, I'm so happy you're staying. I've readied your old room, though I was thinking…you might…consider…your grandmother's room. It's the biggest in the house and has a wonderful view of the bridge. I know she would have been happy for you to use it for your own."

Mary looked up in surprise. It pained her to imagine staying in her grandmother's bedroom. She would have to think about it. She looked down into her teacup and felt lost. "I might take a look at the art studio tonight. It's been a while."

Margaret smiled understandingly. "I thought you might." She nodded. You and your grandmother spent a lot of time in there."

The fog touched the kitchen windows as the sun began to set in the west. Mary stifled a yawn and stretched. "The day wore me out more than I realized. I think I might get settled and unpack my clothes."

"That sounds smart, dear. There's some dinner warming in the oven. Joseph and I will be down in our cottage in a bit. Give us a ring if you need anything."

"Thank you, Margaret. It…really is good to be home." She smiled.

Mary leaned over and gave her a quick hug. She breathed in the scent of rose petals. She lifted her overnight bag over her shoulder and moved toward the staircase closest to the kitchen.

Mary climbed the spiraling stairs. Framed photographs lined the walls. Some were as old as the house itself. Each step captured another year, another decade. Precious memories captured in gilded frames. As she reached the top step, her eyes were drawn to a small photograph, Mary and her mother enjoying an afternoon at Pier 39, their arms wrapped around one another as they smiled for the camera. Sea lions slept peacefully in the sun, basking behind them on wooden docks. So many precious moments slip by, lost forever. What she wouldn't give to have her mother's arms around her now, to hear her laugh. She would even welcome the old arguments. They'd had some big ones over the years. She smiled sadly. Anything would be better than feeling her absence—that cold silence. The desire to see her mother's face was overwhelming. She pushed through the moment of pain, trying her best to endure it. The waves of grief were relentless. She took a deep breath and looked over the stair rail. She noticed the large chandelier above the parlor. A breeze blew past her face and the crystals jingled like soft laughter.

She made her way down the dark hallway, past framed oil paintings dating back to 1870. The largest canvas displayed the Embarcadero Train Station. Several horse drawn carriages waited the arrival of passengers. The frames matched the dark mahogany doors, which opened to bedrooms and baths. The rooms were closed to trap in the heat. The last door at the end of the hall led to a bedroom. Turning the crystal knob, she made her way inside the cold room. Everything was just as she'd left it. Mementos from her childhood—stuffed animals, porcelain dolls, and Breyer horses arranged neatly along the walls. She walked over to the cherry wood bookshelf and looked at her old novels, *Black Beauty, Nancy Drew, The Lion, The Witch, and The Wardrobe.*

She smiled as she held *Black Beauty*. The pages were worn, the corners bent. Raindrops pattered softly against the bedroom window. She walked over and lifted the glass a few inches, inhaling the crisp, clean air, a partial view of the Golden Gate Bridge in the distance. A thick blanket of fog obscured it. She turned away, her eyes drifting toward the wardrobe in the corner of the room. The cherry wood antique was recently polished. The furniture was as old as the home. She marveled at how Margaret maintained the house so beautifully. Mary often asked her to take it easy and she always laughed and echoed her husband's words, *Working keeps me healthy and out of trouble.* Mary opened the wardrobe and the wood creaked on its hinges. The aroma of Old English and mothballs filled the air. She sorted through her tote bag and hung her clothes for the next day.

Something caught her eye on the top shelf, an old music box. She reached for it. A porcelain figure stood with her arms outstretched, ready to dance, her right foot peeking out from beneath a blue ball gown. Mary turned the golden key in the back. Music chimed as the Victorian lady twirled in a graceful circle.

Casey would waltz with a strawberry blond
And the band played on.
He'd glide 'cross the floor with the girl he adored
And the band played on.
But his brain was so loaded it nearly exploded,
The poor girl would shake with alarm.
He'd ne'er leave the girl with the strawberry curls
And the band played on.

She smiled as the notes slowly came to an end. The song had been her grandmother's favorite. She carried the music box and placed it at the top of the nightstand.

Darkness drifted into the room. She switched on the lamp next to the bed, an old Tiffany with bright pink roses. The soft light was comforting. She was inclined to climb into bed and read one of her old books, perhaps *Black Beauty*, for old time's sake, but resisted the urge. Mary quickly undressed, slipping on a comfortable pair of pajamas and slippers, and headed out of the bedroom down the hall, passing the collection of vintage paintings. The wind shook the trees surrounding the house. Branches raked the mansion's walls. The hall was dark. She flipped an overhead switch. Her slippers padded down the marble floors until she found herself standing in front of the old art studio. A flood of memories surfaced as she entered the room.

Relax your grip, Mary. Her grandmother gently placed her wrinkled hand over hers. *Long, sweeping strokes. No worries. There are no mistakes in art. Remember?* She smiled. *It all comes from here,* she pointed to the child's heart. *Draw what you feel.*

Mary studied the teddy bear sitting on the table. She looked at the soft, cinnamon fur and took a deep breath, biting down onto her bottom lip in concentration. Slowly her pencil moved across the page. Before she knew it, the stuffed animal's likeness appeared on paper. A smile lit up her face. It was just like a magic trick.

There you see! You have the gift. You're an artist. Her grandmother grinned proudly. Mary smiled back. She looked up, her heart filled with wonder.

She fumbled for the light switch until the shadows were banished to the corners of the room.

The old studio had stayed pretty much the same. A large bay window was at the back of the spacious room. She opened the curtains and was greeted by fog encased city lights. The winds howled and branches swayed as the evening's storm picked up energy.

Her eyes wandered over the paintings on the walls. A collection of oil and acrylic canvases created over the years. The back window set up two easels. She noticed the one closest to her held an unfinished painting. Mary peered down at the long, sweeping brushstrokes. A partially completed face gazed back. Large blue eyes peered under thick lashes. She would have known those eyes anywhere. It was a portrait of her Great Grandmother, Mara. Mary knew the artist at once. It was obviously her Grandmother Helen's work. She recognized the delicate brushstrokes at a glance. When did she start this painting? She always shared her art projects with her. Why not this time?

She realized her grandmother would never finish the painting. A tightening sensation gripped her throat. When the tears rose, she didn't fight them. She slid down to the floor and wept, her body shaking uncontrollably.

Eventually, she managed to sit up, roughly wiping away the tears. As she regained her composure, a glint of metal caught her eye. She reached down and touched the small, gold object on the floor. It was cold to the touch. The shiny key was about an inch long and felt heavy in her hand. She looked up at the wooden table, to the right of the easel. The oil on the palette looked fresh. It wasn't like her grandmother to leave her work area without cleaning up afterwards. She shook her head from side to side wondering if she'd been painting on the day she died. If this was the case, at least she was doing what she loved most. Next to the palette was an old, leather bound book. She examined the worn material. The edges of the pages were gold leaf. There was a lock on the far right side of the cover. She hesitated for a moment. If it was a diary, perhaps she should leave it alone. She stood in silence biting her lower lip. In the end, her curiosity was too strong to resist the temptation, with a trembling hand, she placed the key in the lock. For a moment nothing happened. The metal rattled. There was a click, and the bound pages opened to her past. The scent of dried roses lingered in the air.

Chapter 2

Mary eyed the ivory pages—delicate handwriting yellowed with age.

This diary belongs to Mara Elizabeth McClain. November 4th, 1870, the Year of Our Lord.

Mary exhaled slowly. Her heart drummed as she realized that the diary belonged to her great-grandmother. McClain had been her maiden name. Her eyes moved back and forth over the page.

As I write these words, my hands are shaking. I arrived in the town of Oakland in the late afternoon. Soon after, a ferry brought me to San Francisco. The train ride was tedious. There was something wrong with the brakes. My stomach lurched every time we came to a stop. Little did I know this would be the least of my worries. Had I known the dangers of my newly adopted city, would I have dared to make this journey? I'm not certain. Although today was by far the strangest of my life, it did possess some magical moments. I fear that my very soul was shaken. These feelings are so overwhelming. Were there really flecks of gold in those velvety brown eyes? I was lost in his gaze. Looking at his face was like falling through space and time. His smile was gentle, playful, but honestly, really quite forward. It's not like we are old friends after all! He's a complete stranger. Honestly, it was really quite presumptuous of him to look at me so. Part of me wanted to run, to flee, another part wanted, well, something else entirely…

Her words were like gentle brushstrokes. Mary was vaguely aware of the art studio. She could hear the whistle of the train engine, the pounding of the rain against the windows. Long sheets spread across the glass distorting the scenery outside. The cold, damp air embraced her. The years rolled backwards and she found herself immersed within the shadows of San Francisco's Gilded Age.

Chapter 3

Her eyes focused intently on her stitches, skilled fingers working the needle, moving rapidly over the cloth. An image of a cottage emerged within the colorful threads. Seven days had passed since her departure from Philadelphia. The train chugged forward, mile after mile it traveled, leaving behind the comforts of home. A sudden bump on the tracks made her pitch occasionally forward. She braced herself, clutching the arms on the leather seat. *Just focus on your sewing, listen to the rain.* Hail pummeled the window in violent sheets. The train car jostled from side to side, teetering on its tracks. Steamy swirls of mist floated by the glass. She let out a deep sigh. Echoes of the past surfaced in her mind. Her mother lying in a pink, satin lined casket. Plump, little hands clasped her beloved Rosary. No longer would she count the prayer beads, patiently reciting Hail Mary's and Our Fathers. Mara's chest tightened at the thought. The embroidery blurred as hot tears stung her eyes. She tried to blink them back. One drop escaped and rolled down her rosy cheek. She brushed it away like an annoying insect. Crying was useless. She had to stay in control. The train would soon arrive in Oakland.

Her inheritance would hold her over for a few months, she planned to invest most of her money into her business. Mara had reached out by letter to various rental homes in San Francisco. She'd been corresponding with a Mrs. Sarah Levy, a widow who owned a well-known boarding house in the city. The room was described as modest but affordable. Mara did not require much, only a clean space for a bed, a window to write by, and a safe haven. The matron would provide meals.

It was a leap of faith. She knew it. Opening an art gallery was a gamble. Would she find customers? She needed to procure a variety of artworks. So much was at stake. She'd reached out to dozens of art patrons over the past several months. There were few responses. *Would anyone be interested in her gallery?*

She would have to wait and see. Hopefully, she would figure it all out before her money ran out. Failure was not an option. She tried to push her worries to the back of her mind. *Just take it one day at a time.* The train whistle shrieked as it rolled towards Oakland Depot.

The passengers rose from their seats, collecting their bags and pocketbooks. Everyone was anxious to leave, to board the ferry over to San Francisco. Eager travelers pushed toward the dock. Icy winds chilled her body as she waited in line. A young man working on deck offered his hand and helped her climb the slippery steps. Mara found a seat near the front. A crimson sky swirled blood-colored streaks onto the swirling currents. Her eyes were heavy as the ferry made its way to San Francisco's Embarcadero. She was beginning to drift off when she heard the captain announcing their arrival. Once again, she gathered her bags and made her way outside. The rain had tapered to a light drizzle, but the wind was cold and gave her a shock. She walked down a ramp leading to a covered building, and then stood for a moment looking out at the hazy street. She moved into the darkness, slowly, reluctant. Some boys began lighting street lamps and her eyes gradually adjusted to the muted light. By the time she made her way over to the parked carriages, they were already occupied. Eager families were loaded inside, ready to be on their way. An elderly driver called down from his buggy.

"Miss, there will be some more cabs arriving in the next half hour if you don't mind waiting."

The crowd had dwindled. Mara found herself alone on the quiet street. She lifted her silk dress as she walked, trying to avoid the mud and puddles. The odor of horse manure was heavy, the street littered with debris. A cool breeze touched her face as she searched for a dry patch of ground to set her bags. She looked up at the foggy sky. A sliver of moonlight slipped through the cloud cover illuminating the street. The wind whipped, making her eyes water. She pulled her overcoat tightly against her body, shivering.

A man appeared from the shadows. He watched in silence. Swiftly, he closed the distance, the sound of his feet concealed by the roar of the wind. Mara felt the heavy grip of his hands on her shoulders. Startled, she turned around. Greasy hair hung in his eyes. Rusty tobacco stains yellowed his graying beard. A smile moved over his leathery face.

"Well, little girly, are you lost? Do you need an escort?" he snickered. The sound of his voice sent a chill down her spine. Her throat tightened. He grabbed at her arms and began pulling her in the direction of the dark alley. As he pushed her into the shadows, she struggled, tripping over her feet, slipping in the mud. Her muffled screams drowned out by the roar of the wind.

"Let go of me!"

"Welcome to San Francisco, sweetness." He shoved her down onto the cold cobblestones, eyes leering, his hands pushing up her dress. The air was heavy with the odor of dried sweat and stale tobacco. The sound of her beating heart roared in her ears.

And yet a sudden calm washed over her. She could hear the din of her mother's voice in the wind. *A lady must always be ready to protect herself. Wake up, Mara!* Her right hand reached back to her bonnet, frantically searching. At first her fingers fumbled in vain, but she eventually managed to retrieve the sharp hatpin wedged through the velvet cloth. The long needle hovered for a moment before finding its target. She stabbed it forcefully into his bulbous nose and yanked it back with a soft pop. A stream of blood flowed forth from the wound. He bellowed in pain, retreating with his hands over his face.

"You stupid little bitch!"

Mara managed to get back on her feet, her legs trembling. His eyes blazed with fury and he lunged toward her. She raised the pin in front of his face.

"Any closer and I'll stab you in the eye. God help me, I will!"

Suddenly he was yanked backwards into the fog. A young man had him by the shoulder, turning him around. He pulled his arm back and punched him across the jaw. His head went backwards in an arch, and his figure collapsed into a motionless heap in the mud.

"Are you hurt, miss?" The man looked anxiously at Mara, and then moved closer, placing his hands gently around her waist to steady her. She looked up into his dark eyes. Her legs were weak from shock and didn't feel as if they belonged to her. The ground under her feet seemed to be moving.

"I'm alright, I think. Thank you," she answered, her voice faraway and low.

When he was certain she could stand her own, he stepped back, looking down into her soft blue eyes.

"I was just getting ready to ride home, and I heard your screams from the gym." He pointed toward the street with a hand wrapped in white tape. "I'm not sure if you really needed my help," he chuckled softly. "You had him on the ropes, lass," he said. "I don't think he expected a young lady to be armed." He looked down at the hatpin she was still clutching. Mara vaguely noticed his Irish accent. His voice was warm and soothing, drifting in from a distance. It seemed as if she had fallen into a strange dream.

"Are you waiting for a cab? This is a dangerous area for an unescorted woman."

"Yes. I…" she stammered. "I'm waiting for a cab. They were all occupied when I left the ferry. I think I lost my bags."

The young man noticed them in the middle of the street. He quickly walked over and retrieved them. "I'd be happy to wait with you. You do seem a bit shaken if you don't mind my saying so." His eyes were gentle.

"Thank you very much, sir."

"My name is Patrick Deane. And may I ask your name?"

"Mara McClain."

A smile moved over his face. "Well now. That's about as Irish as they come," he said.

"Yes," she answered slowly. "My grandparents came here from Ireland." Her words seemed far away.

"Did you hurt your hands?" She looked down at his bandages.

"My hands?" he asked puzzled, then understanding, "Oh, the wraps. No. My hands are fine. The cloth helps to protect my fingers when I'm sparring."

She looked up perplexed. She wanted to leave for the boarding house, away from this alley and its cold confusion. He studied her face, his dark hair scattering over top his forehead, falling into his eyes. He moved a few stray strands away with his taped hand.

His fixed gaze made her uncomfortable and she began speaking too fast. "I need to find Mrs. Levy's Boarding house. I believe it's on O'Farrell Street," she replied, pointing down the cobblestone road.

His eyes flickered with a touch of mischief. He chuckled softly, "Yes. That's right, darlin'." Dimples surfaced around his mouth as he smiled. "Miss McClain, I happen to be very familiar with that side of town."

Mara was not sure why this was so amusing. She looked up at his face. His skin was quite fair in contrast to his dark hair. Thick, black lashes framed vibrant brown eyes, flecks of gold radiating around the pupils. The color was intense, mysterious. She wanted to keep looking, but thought it rude to stare. Instead, she turned way, studying the street, searching for another carriage.

"I can follow alongside your cab when it arrives. I have my horse saddled up around the corner. I'd be happy to escort you over to the Levy house. I'm heading over there myself."

"You are?"

"Yes," he said, smiling. "It's my home." His eyes shone with amusement, looking down at Mara's bewildered face.

"You live there?" She asked in astonishment.

He looked at her patiently. "Well, yes, Miss McClain. You know that it's a boarding house, right? I just so happen to be one of the boarders," he said, grinning. Mara barely heard the carriage pulling up alongside her.

"Looks like your chariot has arrived," he said. "The young lady would like a ride to the Levy Boarding House on O'Farrell Street." He handed the driver some coins.

"Oh, Mr. Deane, I can pay my own way."

"I'm sure you can, Miss McClain, but I'd like to take care of this one for you." he said firmly.

Patrick finished paying the driver and turned to Mara offering his arm. As she took it, she felt his firm muscles against her body. Her face flushed. She pushed a locket of strawberry blond hair behind her ear, a nervous habit. Once she was seated, he helped the driver with the bags and grinned up at her. "I'll see yah back at Miss Levy's house." he said with a wink.

"Thank you, Mr. Deane."

She watched him disappear into the fog and wondered if she'd imagined him: lost in thought, the carriage made its way down the cobblestone road.

Chapter 4

The horses moved in unison, blowing vapors of steam into the cold night air. A black gelding trotted on the left side, while a petite sorrel mare pulled on the right. They both appeared underweight, their ribs jutting painfully beneath glistening coats. Their heads were held rigidly by bearing reins, locked in a severe upright angle. They headed east, eventually making their way down Kearny Street. Mara looked out her carriage window. Loud, celebratory voices echoed from the open doors, passing saloons and gambling houses. The air was heavy with cigar smoke and perfume. A team of horses crossed their path, and they stopped momentarily in front of a two-story building covered in bright pink paint. A large sign outside read, *Lola's Ladies*.

Scantily clad women paced the building's balcony, waving and throwing kisses to the eager men below. A dark haired woman leaned over the railing, bending seductively to show off her well-endowed figure. She dropped a pink silk handkerchief over the balcony. It drifted lazily down toward the sidewalk. Two young men rushed for it, fighting over the treasure. The taller of the two caught the linen, but his companion snatched it out of his hand and he made his way inside the pink hotel.

Mara wondered if this was one of the city's famed houses of ill repute. She had read about such places, never imagining she would see one in person. The carriage continued its slow pace, passing dining halls, saloons, and boarding houses. One building had a sign above the entrance that read, *The Golden Queen*. The door was open, allowing a glimpse inside. Men were gathered around various card tables. An attractive woman was dealing near the front entrance. Golden curls bounced down over her shoulders as she shuffled the deck. Her hands moved expertly over the hearts and diamonds, the cards floating down like the wings of a dove.

After a couple blocks, the buildings became refined in appearance. Several restaurants and hotels were open for business. Fancy carriages and well-bred horses lined the street. Dignified looking gentlemen escorted sophisticated ladies dressed in the latest fashions. Silk dresses layered in embroidered ruffles fluttered gracefully in the wind. Restaurant windows displayed silhouettes of couples illuminated by soft candlelight.

The carriage turned onto California Street and began making its way up the steep road. Overgrown hooves slipped along the cobblestones. Halfway up the street, the horses lost their footing, and the tug of gravity pulled them backwards. For a terrible moment it appeared they were going to roll back down the hill. The driver brought out a long switch of black leather and whipped it hard across their rumps, while saying "Move, you worthless beasts."

They snorted, struggled, and eventually managed to get the carriage moving forward again. Mara was relieved that they'd gained their balance, and at the same time horrified by the cruel treatment of the animals. Halfway up, the buggy made a left turn, making its way toward O'Farrell Street. Mr. Deane was waiting outside a large, two-story house, an elderly horse was tied to a hitching post in front of the white picket fence. Patrick quickly made his way over to the carriage and helped Mara with her bags.

Once outside, she headed straight to the driver's horses. Beads of blood and perspiration covered their sweat-soaked coats. Several angry welts rose over their rumps. She reached up, gently stroking the hot neck of the black gelding. He eyed her softly.

She turned to the driver in anger. "Sir, your horses have scars up and down their flanks. I can see their ribs sticking out plain as day." She pointed with her gloved hand. "When's the last time they've eaten or rested? You really should take better care of your animals! They're God's creatures after all."

The driver's mouth drew down in a grimace. His eyes narrowed, he began to reply, but took one look at Patrick and changed his mind. He yanked the reins, and the team disappeared into the fog. Mara listened sadly to the echo of hoof beats fading into the wind.

Patrick looked at the young woman with surprised admiration. "Well, you're a regular little firecracker," he chuckled softly, but he sobered when he noticed the tears in her eyes. "You're absolutely right, my dear. Animals were not put down on this earth to be abused and neglected. They deserve our respect," he said. "Just look at Sammy over there." He walked over to the dapple-gray gelding. The elderly horse had a refined head, shiny silver mane, and intelligent looking eyes.

Patrick stroked its shoulder as the horse nibbled at his coat. "Don't know what I'd do without my old friend." He reached into his coat pocket and offered him a sugar cube. Sammy greedily took it from his hand, nudging him for more.

"Oh my, he's a handsome fellow," Mara said. She looked up at Patrick's face, startled once again by his smoldering eyes. She looked away before she lost herself in his gaze. "Do you mind if I pet him?"

"Of course. My boy loves the pretty ladies."

Mara blushed. For a moment she wondered if Patrick brought Sammy around many pretty ladies. She imagined that he probably did. She couldn't have been the first woman to notice Mr. Deane's handsome face.

"Oh, yes, Sammy is a good old boy. I should get him set up in the paddock with his dinner, but let's get you settled inside first."

He took her bags and walked to the front porch. Two white columns surrounded the entryway. A wooden swing sat underneath a large arch window. Colorful flowerpots swayed under the eaves. A middle-age woman opened the front door and smiled, and the aroma of baked goods drifted past. Mara's stomach rumbled in hunger. Patrick introduced Mara to Mrs. Sarah Levy. Thick, gold-rimmed spectacles magnified dark blue eyes. Her salt and pepper hair was done up in a large bun. A floral apron was tied around her plump waist.

Patrick gave Mrs. Levy a quick retelling of the incident at the Embarcadero. Her eyes widened as he described Mara holding her own against the assailant with her hatpin.

"Oh, my poor girl. Just arrived in the city and you're already fighting for your life! San Francisco is becoming overrun with meshugas."

Mara looked up, startled.

"What I mean to say is…well…there are crazy, dangerous people everywhere in this town. You have to be careful. I'm glad you know how to protect yourself." She smiled approvingly. "Sounds like you have a good head on your shoulders. And a pretty one too! Come on in and warm yourself by the fire."

Mrs. Levy led Mara to a large fireplace at the back of the parlor where family photographs covered the mantel. The warmth of the flames eased her shivering body. "My grandson, David, will bring your bags up for you." A few moments later, a tall, lanky boy came down the steps. He had a mop of curly hair and dark blue eyes like his grandmother. He smiled shyly and introduced himself. His polite, easygoing attitude made Mara take to him at once. They took a quick tour of the bottom floor, which lead to a comfortable parlor, dining room and kitchen.

"Would you like a cup of tea, Miss McClain?"

"Oh, that would be wonderful. Thank you."

Mrs. Levy brought over two porcelain cups from the cupboard and set them on a table in the kitchen. Both women took their seats

"Your house is lovely."

"Oh, I'm glad you like it. I don't like to boast, but we do have one of the finest boarding homes in town. My husband, Jacob, God rest his soul, built it with his own two hands." She smiled proudly. Miss Levy poured steaming tea into the cups, offering cream and sugar.

"How long have you lived in San Francisco?"

"Oh, well, let me see. A while. Our journey started in the spring of 1850. We traveled by covered wagon, down the California Trail. There was no choice but to sell most of our belongings before the trip. The load needed to be light, it's hard on the horses otherwise." She smiled with a far off look.

Mara nodded with interest. Mrs. Levy took a deep breath and went on.

"My husband and I were newlyweds, just starting out on our own. Mr. Levy had recently inherited some savings from his father. It gave us the means to travel and start over in a new city. We decided to try our luck in San Francisco. There was so much to do before we left; we had to pare down our possessions for the long wagon ride. We discussed what was most important to us—what to sell, what to give away, what to keep. My husband brought along his carpentry tools packed in an old cedar chest. Mr. Levy came from a long line of carpenters. Many generations of Levy practiced the trade. He'd worked with his father in the family business back in our hometown in Idaho.

"Well, I brought along my hope chest, a wedding present. Inside were a few family quilts, photographs, my wedding dress, and an antique silver brush and mirror. I had three homespun dresses, which I washed between wearing. The wagon train often camped by rivers and lakes along the trail. We used the water for cooking, bathing, and cleaning. It was quite an adventure, and a long, difficult journey. My husband and I had joined a wagon train over near Fort Hall along the Snake River. It's good that we left when we did. We were able to bypass some storms that season.

"We made sure to time our trip so we wouldn't be caught in the snow. You see there was a terrible incident that took place back in '46. This was a few years before our journey. A group of travelers were trapped by a heavy snowfall in Truckee, in the Sierra Nevada Mountains. I believe they called themselves *The Donner-Reed Party,* if I remember correctly. Their wagons couldn't get through the storm. The poor souls were low on supplies. Quite a few starved to death. Only about half of them made it to California. Good Lord, I heard that some of the travelers resorted to cannibalism." She shuddered. "Thankfully, we were luckier than that. We left earlier in the season and avoided most of the heavier snow.

"We traveled along the California Trail, through the Nevada desert, down the Sierra Nevada Range. Oh, the heat was terrible in the desert. It was more than anything we could have ever imagined. Afterwards we boasted that we had seen the elephant, meaning we hit some hard traveling for sure.

"So many stories…good and bad, but I'll have to wait to tell you about those tales another day," she smiled.

"It was such a relief when we finally made it to San Francisco. We were both exhausted from the journey, but no sooner had we arrived than I began to wonder if we had made a terrible mistake."

Mara added a splash of cream to her cup with a spoonful of sugar. She blew away the steam as Miss Levy continued her tale.

"The little town of San Francisco had grown from a few hundred residents to over twenty-five thousand by the time we had arrived in the spring of 1850. California had recently joined statehood in the Union. It was such an amazing time. I'm sure you're familiar with all of the exciting stories of the 49ers seeking their fortunes. People sure did have the Gold Fever."

"Yes. I've read about the Gold Rush in newspapers back home," Mara remarked.

"Everyone had dreams of striking it rich in the Sacramento River, down by Sutter's Mill. Businesses were thriving in San Francisco. There were makeshift hotels, gambling halls, and mercantile stores. Entrepreneurs were eager to take advantage of all the new arrivals and their gold dust. Oh, dear, there were even brothels being built. Everything was so strange and exotic compared to our hometown."

Mara nodded and smiled. She took a sip of tea. "My cab passed a building called Lola's Ladies," she said blushing. "I've never seen anything quite like it."

Mrs. Levy rolled her eyes and nodded.

"Did you and your husband ever try to mine for gold?" Mara asked.

"Oh, no, dear. Thank goodness Mr. Levy never had any interest in gold hunting. He had another idea on how to make our fortune. When we first arrived, we met families returning from the Sacramento Valley. They told us stories of their gold seeking adventures and some were quite disturbing. The winter of '49 was harsh. Miners suffered from the elements, from cold and disease. Vegetables and fruit were hard to come by. Scurvy struck many of them. Some were so weak they could barely walk. The miners risked their lives when they made their way back to San Francisco.

"Robbers would sometimes ambush them along the trail. They hid their gold dust under horse saddles, in food containers, coffee pots. You name it. We met one family who told us that they had bagged up some of their gold and hid it inside their toddler's diaper. Oh, my goodness. Can you imagine? What a crazy time.

"The men that returned all had different stories. Some came back with real fortunes. Others were destitute. Some prospectors wanted to settle down after their first trip to Sacramento. Some struck it rich and then lost their money in the city's gambling halls or by other foolish ventures. They would return to Sacramento and start all over again, but gold mining was not an easy way of life. You know, it's funny; I think the smartest ones were the shopkeepers. They sold supplies to the miners. The prices went up as more and more people arrived into town. I heard they were selling picks and shovels for bags of gold dust. The merchants were richer than the gold prospectors!"

"Well, anyway, when they returned, housing was difficult to find, sometimes impossible. There were a few hotels, mostly pre-fab buildings; most of them with just sheets separating the rooms. People leased out all kinds of places to sleep in or on. I even heard some rented saw horses for beds! The miners took what they could get. They were desperate. And oh, the prices they charged the renters! Obscene! Some places would charge by the cot. Strips of muslin dividing rooms, if they were divided at all. Privacy was a rare find. And people were willing to pay just about anything, even for an old dirty mattress. Oh Lord, and there were vermin too. Lice, fleas, rodents. She shuddered. "People had to cover themselves up so the rats wouldn't bite them in their sleep. It was so awful.

"My husband's predictions came true. Lodgings were few and far between. Word got round about his carpentry skills. Soon, families were offering gold dust to help build their homes, sometimes even gold nuggets! Can you imagine?

"Well our first few years were definitely challenging, but we were lucky compared to most. My husband and I were able to purchase a nice plot of land. It's the same lot where our house rests today. We'd become good friends with a family in the neighborhood. They were fed up with the wild lifestyle of San Francisco. The husband did quite well for himself mining. They tried to settle down in the city but changed their minds after a few months and wanted to move back east. They sold us their land for pennies on the dollar. We were humbled. And it was lucky we purchased when we did. Real-estate prices were becoming outrageous.

"Jacob set up a tent with spruce beams and thick canvas—just one large room. He built us a bed, a table—bought us a small stove. We kept it outside underneath an awning. There was a wooden outhouse in the backyard and another small tent to do our washing and bathing. My husband added a paddock for our horses to shelter them too. He was so busy building those first few months he barely had time to sleep.

"Eventually, everything started to take shape. It was pretty dry that first summer, dust everywhere, on our clothes, the furniture, even our food. You'd wipe it down and it would come back the same day. We prayed for rain. Our prayers were answered, but the relief didn't last long. Then came the mud. The constant traffic of men, animals, wagons cutting up the streets to make giant sinkholes. Why, you were in danger of sinking and never coming back up again! I remember a time when a couple men left one of the saloons up on Kearny Street. They fell into one of the sinkholes and barely made it out alive. I read all about it in the Alta Vista, our one and only news source in the city. The paper was full of crazy stories like that!

"Residents tried to fill in the mud holes. We didn't have anything like them paved streets you see today. The city purchased large quantities of brush in an attempt to fill the muddy roads. City employees would throw it down into the sinkholes, but it didn't help much. People were so desperate for solid ground. All kinds of rubbish tossed into the streets and sidewalks—garbage, old furniture, sinks, you name it. Ground got firmer and walkways were built up over the debris.

"About the same time, ships came in with more people, supplies, and building materials. My husband and his new partner, Isaac Collins, were excited to get to work building new homes, but they ran into a very big problem. They had to find a way to get their supplies. Ship crews were abandoning their vessels to seek their own fortunes in Sacramento. Soon, the beautiful bay had turned into a ship graveyard. The giant hulks were left out to rot where they were anchored. What a sight!

"Well, for a short time, things seemed to settle down. Supplies were eventually brought to shore. Many of the ships never made it back to sea. Some of 'em ended up being used as boarding houses and stores after they were hauled to shore. Gold dust was flowing into town. Jobs were abundant. Anyone willing to work could get hired.

"My husband and his partner started building pre-fab houses. Their first homes were simple constructions, square boxes really, but they were better than the makeshift tents and shanty rooms many of the residents were living in around town. They hired a nice crew and soon had several homes going up at once, including ours. We added onto our home as the business grew. I can't tell you what a joy it was to have solid walls again! Homes in our neighborhood were springing up around us. We made friends with a couple of families in the area. Now, at the time, men far outnumbered women and children. It was always nice when you could find a family to spend time with…like our neighbor, Rachel Connor.

"Her husband worked at the mercantile down the street. They had a young daughter and another on the way. The poor family was sleeping in a drafty tent downtown. It was heartbreaking; I offered them a room for rent. They paid what they could, and Rachel helped around the house, cooking meals and helping with the chores.

"Word spread that we had extra space in our house and we had so many offers. It was nice to be able to pick and choose from the more respectful renters. The lodgers paid nicely, and between my husband's contracted work and our boarders, we were able to continue to build onto our home, eventually fashioning it into the Greek Revival you see today."

"I'm not familiar with the Greek Revival Style," Mara interrupted.

"Well, it was very popular in the fifties. The tiled red roof, stucco walls, front porch and attic are some of the features that make our home unique. All of the bedrooms in our house have large windows with Juliet balconies. The parlor and living areas have arched windows. One of my favorite additions is the column feature surrounding the porch.

"Our neighbors' were quite taken with the design. Mr. Levy was barely finished remodeling our home when the neighbors started asking him to add onto their houses. Yes, we did well in those years. As better building materials became available, my husband and his partner was able to work on more sophisticated architectural projects.

"My husband eventually added a large room underneath our house. It made a wonderful root cellar. I planted a little garden out back. It was a challenge, but I finally managed to purchase a few hens and an old rooster. So we had fresh eggs whenever we wanted. And we were happy to share them with our tenants and the neighbors. The price of eggs was so steep back then, sometimes a dollar an egg! What a luxury!

"Well, pretty soon, Mr. Levy and I fell in love with our girls. They were wonderful pets. We never had the heart to cull them for dinner, even when they stopped laying. Even our old, cranky rooster was safe," she said. "I eventually gave up meat all together. Being Orthodox Jews, we kept to a kosher diet. My husband and I already avoided pork and shellfish. So, giving up the remaining meats wasn't that difficult for us.

"I still have a few hens left, offspring from the original flock. I hope you like eggs, dear. We always provide fresh eggs for breakfasts. I like to think it makes up for not serving meat.

Mara smiled, nodded, "I love fresh eggs. A vegetarian diet sounds interesting. I'll be happy to try it. Do you ever get any complaints from renters about not serving meat?" she asked.

"Every once in awhile I'll hear a grumble or two, but I always explain our policy to the boarders before they lease their rooms. It seems that most of them get used to it fairly quickly. And if they don't, they have a variety of restaurants to choose from around town.

"Well, anyway, Jacob eventually added an upstairs wing with the extra money we earned. Seven bedrooms altogether. We figured that once the children came, our boarding business would end. Yes, we had dreams of filling our home with lots of babies." She smiled sadly. "But, the good lord had other plans. Our daughter, Ruth, was our first and only child.

"My God, it's strange to think of all that happened those first years. You know, I forgot to mentions the fires."

Mara looked up with wide eyes. "I heard there were fires in San Francisco. Did any of them get close to your home?"

"Well dear, we were very lucky. As I said before, hotels and buildings were springing up throughout the city. There were quite a few new constructions on Kearny Street. A devastating fire happened before we arrived. It ignited on the early morning of Christmas Eve, 1849. It started down by the plaza, Dennison Exchange, and made its way down Kearny and Washington, eventually down to Montgomery Street—took out homes, hotels, gambling halls. Many lives were lost and people injured, but an even bigger fire was set in the spring off '50.

"My family and I were very fortunate. The fires didn't reach our neighborhood. We found out later that arsonists were responsible. It was an opportunity to loot and cause chaos. The townspeople were angry and wanted them punished, but justice didn't come soon enough. Eventually, a group of citizens decided to take matters into their own hands. They called themselves The San Francisco Committee of Vigilance. Suspects were being rounded up, tried, and sentenced the same day. Men were hung in the town's square. It was a terrible time of violence and unrest.

"Life in San Francisco seemed to be settling down the last few years, but then the trains arrived. Now, we're dealing with a whole new danger," she sighed.

"What danger is that?" Mara asked in fascination, sipping her last drop of tea, eager to learn about her newly adopted city. She had no idea she would be getting so many facts on her first night.

"Well," Mrs. Levy answered sadly, "the problems are old ones—ignorance and prejudice.

"Chinese laborers are being blamed for the rising unemployment in this town. The same kind of thing happened to Spanish-Americans during the Gold Rush. There were terrible crimes against them during those first few years. You see, they were seen as a threat, that the Spanish miners were competing for the gold.

"Well, it appears that history is starting to repeat itself. Currently, there are too many residents for the jobs available. As I mentioned earlier, businesses used to be desperate for workers during the Gold Rush. Anyone could find a job if they tried, but the trains changed all that. The population is growing daily and jobs are scarce. Many San Francisco businesses have hired Chinese laborers for low wages and long hours. This is not sitting well with some workers. There was a terrible incident earlier this week. The Waterfront found a young Chinese railroad employee, the back of his head bashed in. His body washed ashore in the early morning." She shuddered. "Oh, dear, I'm sorry. I don't want to frighten you with all this on your first night. Once I start telling stories, it's hard for me to stop.

"Miss McClain, I could tell from your letters that you're an educated young lady. We've always prided ourselves to renting to respectful citizens. Let me show you to your room, dear. I'm sure you need some time to relax after your long day."

They headed upstairs, making their way down a long hallway. Mrs. Levy took a key from her apron pocket and let them into the room. Mara was surprised. A fireplace rested in front of a full size bed, covered neatly with a homespun lavender quilt. There was an oak wardrobe and matching desk. It was adjacent to a small vanity with ceramic washbowl. Waterfront paintings hung on the cream and lavender flowered wallpaper. She parted the calico curtains, covering the large bay window, and looked out onto the gas-lit sidewalk. Several couples were strolling along, perhaps on their way to dinner or the theater.

"The room is beautiful."

"Oh, I'm glad that you like it, dear. Here's your key. I hope you enjoy your stay with us. I should let you get to your unpacking. I'll have supper ready soon. I'm making a batch of latke pancakes tonight. Take your time and make yourself comfortable. Dinner'll be ready at seven." She smiled and let herself out of the room, quietly closing the door behind her.

Chapter 5

The sudden privacy was comforting. Mara walked to the wardrobe and unpacked her clothes. She washed her face over a gold-rimmed washbowl and changed into a soft, sea foam silk dress fringed with white lace. The soft fabric flowed gracefully around her tiny waist. She adjusted the small bustle in the back, turning to look at her reflection in the vanity. Her eyes were glowing. Her stomach tightened when she thought about meeting her new housemates.

At seven, she made her way down the stairs, to the formal dining room. She was startled to see that many of the guests were already seated. The men at the table quickly stood up as she entered. She caught the admiring smile of Patrick Deane. He looked quite handsome in his white silk shirt, navy vest and trousers. His dark hair was brushed neatly back, a couple of waves falling over his forehead.

To his left was a middle-aged man with silver hair and light hazel eyes.

"Hello ma'm, I'm Jeremiah Smith. This is my partner Donald Becker."

The gentleman appeared to be about ten years younger, with a boyish face, and light brown hair. They offered warm smiles as they were introduced. "We have a little mercantile store at the end of the block. We're doing some renovations to the upstairs. That's why we've been staying with Mrs. Levy. It's been a wonderful escape from all the dust and construction."

Donald Becker shook his head. "You would not believe the aggravation of having the upstairs remodeled. I don't know what we'd have done without Mrs. Levy to save the day."

Jeremiah, smiled. "Oh now, just think how nice the new quarters will be when the construction is finished, Donald. Patience."

"It's true, Jerry. You always have a way of putting things in perspective," he said.

Jeremiah continued, "But our store is open for business if you need to stock up after your trip. I know how dreadful moving can be."

"Oh, yes, that'd be wonderful, Mr. Smith. Do you by chance sell art supplies?"

"We do. I happen to enjoy painting myself. I'm quite fond of watercolors. Are you an artist, dear?"

"Well, yes, I like to think of myself as an artist," she answered modestly. "I'm planning on opening an art gallery downtown. I'm hoping to find an affordable place to lease."

Jeremiah and Donald quickly exchanged excited looks.

Donald remarked, "Oh, we'd be happy to help with your grand opening, young lady! You just let us know what you need and we will be happy to help plan the event!"

As they discussed the gallery, Mara noticed a dark haired girl sitting to the right of Patrick Deane. She had a pretty face, dark eyes, and a sensual mouth. Her shapely figure was set off nicely in a rose colored taffeta dress. The color complimented her brunette curls. She listened with a tight smile.

Mrs. Levy politely introduced the young woman. "Miss McClain, this is Miss Jane Darby; she's attending a private finishing school downtown. Miss Darby recently moved from Atlanta."

The young woman smirked, eyeing Mara with distaste.

Mrs. Levy went on, "I was just telling everyone how bravely you fought off that terrible man at the Embarcadero. What a relief it must have been when Mr. Deane showed up!"

The men at the table nodded in admiration.

Miss Darby leaned towards Patrick, softly stroking his shoulder with her cotton glove. In a silky, Southern voice she giggled, "You're always picking up the strays of the city, sugar. Just like that old horse of yours."

Patrick looked uncomfortable and quickly changed the subject. "Miss McClain, have you met Miss Betty Lowe? She owns a bookstore on Powell Street."

"Oh?" Mara perked up. "I would love to visit your shop, Miss Lowe!"

The woman, while in her mid-twenties, appeared much older. She wore a gray calico dress with a high butterfly collar. Her mousy brown hair was drawn back in a tight bun. It looked tight…painful. Large green eyes peered out from thick spectacles, giving her the appearance of a frightened cat.

She smiled shyly. "I'd like that very much. I received some new editions this week, Tolstoy's latest novel, *War and Peace*, arrived yesterday. I have three copies available."

"Really?" Mara answered happily.

Miss Darby rolled her eyes. "How exciting," she said sarcastically.

Miss Lowe's smile faded as she looked down at her plate.

Mara shot Miss Darby an icy look, "It sounds marvelous, Miss Lowe. I plan to come down tomorrow morning. I'd love to purchase a copy."

Miss Lowe's face lit up.

Patrick eyes softened in relief.

A well-dressed man made his way over to the table.

"Sorry, to be so late." Everyone turned and stared. "What a day," he said. Mrs. Levy quickly introduced the young gentleman as Mr. Joshua Cohen. She offered to take his top hat and coat.

"Thank you, Mrs. Levy."

He looked to be in his late twenties, but had the air of someone much older. His gray suit had been recently pressed, leather shoes shined with polish. He took off his top hat, exposing wavy blond hair framing a boyish face. His cheeks were flushed from the cool autumn air.

"I overheard the last part of the conversation when I came in. It's a pleasure to make your acquaintance, Miss McClain." He reached out and took her hand, kissing it gently. Mara noticed that his eyes were an unusual shade of blue, almost aquamarine in color. He took a seat next to her at the table. "I work for the Bank of Wells Fargo. I'd be happy to help you get your accounts in order, if you need any assistance. And I overheard you mention an interest in leasing a business property?"

"Yes, I am."

"Well, it just so happens that one of my clients is looking for a renter. The place is located just down the street from Miss Lowe's bookstore. You two could be neighbors if the property suits you."

"Thank you, Mr. Cohen. I'd be very interested to meet your client."

"Wonderful. I'll make a point of contacting him tomorrow. It's a fairly small city. We should be able to get you in business before you know it."

Miss Darby stared at Mara with a frozen smile.

"Well, now," Mr. Smith interrupted, "I'm sure Miss McClain must be tired and hungry after her long journey. Why don't we all take our seats and enjoy this wonderful meal," he said.

They said grace and began passing around the bowls of food. Mrs. Levy offered wine from a crystal decanter. Mara took a sip of the rich merlot, which eased her frazzled nerves. Miss Darby passed a bowl of salad to Patrick, batting her eyelashes, smiling coyly. Mara felt the blood rise to her cheeks, and tried her best to hide her distaste for the girl. She couldn't remember ever meeting anyone so rude and unpleasant.

Mara took a bite of the potato latke. It was absolutely delicious. She started on a second, and then grew drowsy from the food and wine. After dinner, people drifted back to their rooms, some to the parlor. Mara tiredly said her goodnights and headed for the stairs. As she stepped up, Patrick was making his way down. She caught his eyes as he grinned.

"Miss McClain, it was very nice meeting you this evening. Please let me know if I can be of service to you as you settle into town. I'd be happy to show you around the city when you're up to it."

"Thank you, Mr. Deane, I'd like that very much. And thank you for assisting me earlier. I'm grateful for it."

"My pleasure, darlin'. Have a good night's sleep."

He watched Mara make her way up the stairs. Once inside the bedroom, she changed into a cotton nightdress and snuggled down under the thick blankets. The logs in the fireplace crackled, rain pattered against the window. After plumping her pillow, she reached for her diary on top of the nightstand, clicked open the lock, and began to write…

Chapter 6

Soft light drifted between the seams of the calico curtains. Mara sat up and stretched. For a moment she was unsure of where she was. Yesterday seemed so far away. She slipped on her robe, gathered her clothes, and found her way to the washroom at the end of the hall. She took a quick bath in the porcelain claw-foot tub. After brushing her teeth, she slipped into a soft pink dress, and then made her way downstairs. The house was empty except for Mrs. Levy.

"Well, hello, dear. Would you like some breakfast?" She called up from the bottom of the steps.

"I'm sorry. I must have overslept," Mara answered.

"Not a problem. You certainly had a right to sleep in after your long day. I have eggs and pancakes if you would like some."

"Thank you so much. That sounds wonderful."

She sat down at the kitchen table, took a bite of the golden eggs, and washed it down with a sip of strong coffee.

"Miss McClain, do you have any plans for today? It's your first morning in San Francisco!"

"Yes, I do. I'd love to visit Miss Lowe's bookstore. It's on Powel Street if I remember correctly?"

"It is. If you are able to wait about half an hour, I can give you a ride. I have some errands this morning, and I'd be happy to drop you off along the way."

"Thank you so much! You're so kind."

After breakfast, Mara brought her plate and mug to the farmers' sink and helped Mrs. Levy with the clean-up. The air was crisp as they made their way outside. A red barn stood in the back of the well-kept yard.

Several chickens hurried past. They stopped a few yards away, eagerly pecking the ground for leftover scratch. A small snail crawled over the dewy grass. A red hen grabbed the mollusk and ran. Her companions rushed after her, eager to steal the coveted prize. An elderly rooster watched the scene in silence.

The women made their way into the barn. Two white mares stood munching hay.

"Hello, Misha and Sasha! How are my pretty girls today?" Ms Levy patted them affectionately.

The horses whinnied.

"Ladies, I'd like you to meet our newest resident, Miss McClain."

"It's a pleasure," Mara giggled.

Mrs. Levy sorted through her tack with an expert hand, carefully fitting the mares with bits, breast collars, and harnesses. Afterwards, she hitched the team to a black surrey.

Mara admired their shiny coats, their dark eyes and silver manes. "They're gorgeous. Oh and please call me Mara."

"All right, and you can call me Sarah."

"You're quite the equestrian," Mara replied.

"Well, I've been around horses all my life. My family had a farm back in Idaho. They're amazing animals. You just have to show them a bit of love and respect and they'll work harder than any creature I know."

"I adore horses. I'd love to learn to care for them."

"You're welcome to help me out in the barn anytime you'd like. I'd be happy to show you the ropes."

"That would be wonderful!"

The ladies climbed inside the surrey. Mrs. Levy rested her work boots on the front board and took up the reins. "Let's go, girls." She gave a gentle flick of the line and they were on their way.

The weather was mild as they drove down O'Farrell Street, the ocean breeze blowing gently. Mrs. Levy pointed out Mr. Smith's mercantile shop. It was a fine looking store with large windows displaying a variety of tools and kitchen appliances. There were several wooden crates filled with fruits and vegetables outside. Mara made a mental note to check out their art supplies later in the week. After a few blocks, they turned right on Market Street, passing carriages along the way. The road stretched from the Embarcadero down to the avenues.

A variety of businesses including a post office, a bank, and a fruit stand stood along the busy street. A young shoeshine boy sat on a wooden box polishing an older gentleman's boots. Another child stood on the corner selling newspapers to passersby. Pedestrians moved over the wooden sidewalks, several carrying parcels in their arms. After a few blocks, they made their way down Powell Street. They stopped in front of a store called, *Great Expectations*. Mara climbed down from the surrey and thanked Sarah for the ride. She made her way over and opened the door. A bell jingled as she crossed the threshold.

Betty Lowe was standing on a ladder arranging books. She wore a dark cotton dress, covered by a work apron. Her hair was pulled back in a tight bun, her green eyes peering through thick lenses. A tentative smile moved over her face. "Miss McClain, how nice to see you," she said softly. She made her way down the ladder with ease.

"What a beautiful store. I hope I'm not interrupting your work. I just wanted to drop in for a bit and see your lovely shop. It's amazing!"

"Thank you. I was just putting away the latest shipment. I've been working all morning. I could use a break. Would you like some coffee?"

"Sounds great."

Betty led Mara to a small table in the back of the store. There was a large thermos, a container of cream and sugar, and a stack of cups. She poured the coffee and took a seat.

"Have you had this store long?" Mara asked.

"Well, it was my father's back in the sixties. He passed away a few years ago, and willed it to me. We both liked reading. He used to tell me the most wonderful stories. You see, my mother passed away when I was a little girl. My father...was my world."

"I'm so sorry for your loss, Miss Lowe. My dad passed away three years ago, my mom earlier this year. It's tough, and it leaves such an empty space."

The women nodded at each other understandingly. Mara was surprised at how easily she was opening up to Miss Lowe.

"Call me Betty, please," she said softly.

"Thank you, and please call me Mara."

"It's a deal." She giggled and suddenly appeared ten years younger.

Mara studied her face and noticed that it was pretty in spite of the severe hair and thick spectacles. Her green eyes were stunning, her features delicate. She imagined that, with her hair down, Betty would look quite attractive, but then again looks were not everything. It's what's on the inside that counts. She turned back to the conversation.

"How'd you wind up boarding with Mrs. Levy? If you don't mind me asking that is."

"I don't mind. My father and I lived in a small house a few blocks from the shop, but I sold it. It was just too painful living there…so many memories. I guess I was depressed, thought I'd surround myself with some new faces. You know, a few of those faces are quite handsome." She blushed looking down at her cup.

Mara smiled back. "I noticed."

"I have to admit that I'm a bit taken with Mr. Cohen. He's very kind and has the nicest manners. He's a real hard worker, too," Betty said quietly.

"He does seem nice. And I have to say that Mr. Deane really helped me out last night. I was so relieved when he showed up. It was so dreadful…what happened at the Embarcadero that is," she said.

Betty looked at her in awe. "You're incredibly brave. I would have probably fainted right there on the street."

"It all happened so fast. I was just…lucky."

"No. You're brave, but I agree that Mr. Deane is very nice. Although you better watch your back around Miss Darby. She's had her eye on him from the moment he moved into the house. She's a mean little thing, too. I noticed she was giving you some hard looks last night."

"Mara frowned at the mention of the girl. "I noticed," she said, wrinkling her nose. "She's quite unpleasant. I'll do my best to avoid her."

"Did you know he was a boxer?"

"A boxer?"

"Yes, well, he's a carpenter by trade, but he works down by the docks doing odd jobs. I guess it's been tough for him finding work. Employment is hard to come by these days. Some businesses don't like to hire the Irish. Isn't that strange? They think the jobs should go to American residents. It's so silly. Mr. Deane and his family suffered terribly during *The Famine*. I've heard him call it, *The Great Hunger*. The people in his village had a horrible time back in the sixties. A blight disease hit their potato crops. People starved all over the island. I guess they're still trying to recover from the devastation of those years; the townspeople had a difficult time paying their rent after the crops failed. His family's landlord did not sympathize apparently. That's what Mr. Deane told me anyway…one evening after dinner. Well, I guess he boxes in his spare time, sometimes in matches down on Kearny Street," she whispered. "He sends his earnings back home whenever he can. His parents and siblings live in a little town called Kinvara."

"Oh, I see… I guess that's why his hands were taped when I met him. He mentioned sparring…I had no idea what he was talking about."

Mara was not sure what to make of this. It was a lot to take in.

"Mara, would you like to see the rest of the store?"

"I'd love to!"

Betty escorted her down the rows of bookshelves. There were a few tables and chairs against the walls. Small lamps rested on top of the tables. Each shelf contained various subjects—history, political science, arts, and philosophy. There were also several aisles with fictional novels organized alphabetically.

"You might like to take a look in this section." She led her down toward a shelf near the front desk. "I have a collection of art books. You know, there are some really interesting new artists in France right now. One of my customers brought back a photograph from Paris. It's an image of his friend's painting. Hold on a minute." She went to her desk, sorting through a pile of paperwork.

"Oh, here it is. Now, of course it's black and white, but you can still see it's quite beautiful, so light and airy. I believe his name is Monet…Claude Monet. I can't imagine you've heard of him. He isn't famous or anything, but I think his painting is quite unique. Of course, I'm no expert. What do you think?"

Mara examined the photograph. It was a simple scene—a countryside, a few bales of hay and the setting sun, but the brushstrokes were unlike anything she had seen before. They were delicate, seeming to move along the canvas. The scene was almost electric. The entire composition was divided by dabs of paint. A moment had been captured, a moment in time.

"Wow. I've never seen anything like it! I'd be happy to display his painting in my gallery, if he ever makes his way to The States. His work is exceptional!"

The jingle of the bell made the women jump. Joshua Cohen hurried into the room.

"Ladies, what a pleasure! I was hoping to borrow a little coffee for my thermos." Betty smiled shyly, avoiding eye contact.

"It looks like I came at the perfect time, Miss McClain. My client, Mr. Williams, is at the bank doing his weekly deposit. He's the one I mentioned last night, the gentleman with the property for lease. If you'd like, I can take you over in my carriage. The bank's just down the street a few blocks. You two could discuss business."

"Oh, I'd like that very much. Thank you."

Betty quietly interrupted, "Mr. Cohen, I can fill your thermos with some fresh coffee."

"Marvelous. I'm desperate. Looks like it's going to be a busy day." She took his empty thermos, without looking up, and returned a few moments later with fresh coffee and a book under her arm.

"Mara, this is the novel I was telling you about last night, Tolstoy's *War and Peace*. We'll call it your welcome gift to San Francisco."

"Thank you so much! You're so thoughtful. I can't wait to read it."

They said their goodbyes and headed for the door. Mr. Cohen escorted Mara over to his modest buggy. A tall, chestnut mare stood waiting. Joshua helped her inside the carriage and they made their way down Market Street. She breathed a sigh of relief. It appeared everything was going to work out just fine.

Chapter 7

Mr. Cohen and Mara talked about leasing properties as they rode along. Everything seemed straightforward. After a few blocks, the carriage pulled up to Wells Fargo Bank. The building was a large brick construction. A teenage boy met them outside and attended to the carriage. The banker offered Mara his arm and escorted her to the door. He led her to a desk where a gentleman was busy chatting with one of the employees.

"Mr. Williams, I'd like you to meet San Francisco's newest entrepreneur, Miss Mara McClain."

The gentleman appeared somber as he was introduced. The businessman was on the shorter side, with pasty skin, and dirty blond hair. He looked to be in his early thirties, though a streak of white ran from his right temple to the back of his head. It was startling and Mara wondered if he had experienced some sort of shock.

She forced a smile on her face and reached out her hand. He took it firmly, lifting it to his lips. His gaze traveled over her face, and then to her body...carefully observing.

"What a pleasure to meet such a lovely young lady, and with such an Irish name." He spoke in a British dialect, pronouncing each word carefully.

"Thank you, Mr. Williams. My grandparents were from Galway."

He narrowed his eyes and tightened his jaw. "Oh, yes, I'm familiar with Galway. My family and I managed tenant farms in a place called Kinvara. I'm afraid things became...well...rather messy during *The Famine*," he said. "Yes, quite messy indeed," he added with a far off look. "It's the reason that I came over to The States. I thought it might be a nice change of scenery."

There was something in his eyes that she didn't like. When he smiled, they were empty and cold. They reminded her of the assailant in the alley.

Mr. Williams seemed to recover himself and began asking questions.

"So, my dear, is there a Mr. McClain that I should speak to concerning your interest in leasing my property?"

"No, there isn't. I plan to lease the property on my own."

A tight smile moved over his face.

"Very well then. Why don't you have a seat and we can get down to business. Mr. Cohen pulled up a leather chair and joined them at the table.

"I assume that you've heard that properties are quite expensive in the city, young lady?"

"Yes, I'm afraid I have."

"Well, we may be able to work something out," he said vaguely.

Mara wasn't sure what this meant. An uneasy feeling washed over her.

"I don't quite…follow?"

Mr. Cohen looked uncomfortable as he listened in on their conversation.

"Well, this property, The Powell Street Property, needs a bit of work. It has some ceiling leaks, needs a little maintenance on the floors. A few other things…small things. If you were able to manage to hire someone to fix these problems…let's just say that I might be willing to reduce the rent."

Mr. Cohen spoke up, "Miss McClain, I have an idea. Patrick Deane is a carpenter by trade."

"Yes, Miss Lowe mentioned that earlier."

"I imagine Patrick could do the repairs, and I'm sure he'd give you a reasonable price for his labor."

Mara worked this over in her mind. Yes, it could possibly work, but was she really comfortable with having this strange man as her landlord? It could present problems down the road.

Mr. Williams studied her face, seeming to sense her hesitation. "Well, dear, you'll need to decide today. I'm afraid there's already been quite a bit of interest in the property." He smiled shrewdly. "I could drive us over and you can take a look yourself."

She looked up anxiously at Mr. Cohen. "Would you be interested in looking at the property as well?"

He smiled apologetically. "I'm afraid I have a one o'clock

appointment, Miss McClain, but I'd be happy to assist you with the paperwork afterwards."

Mara's mind was racing. Every instinct told her to walk away, but in the end, she ignored her feelings.

"Yes, Mr. Williams, I'd like to see your property."

He escorted her outside to the back of the building. A large carriage with two black horses waited. The animals wore heavy blinders, their heads held up tightly. The tails were docked sharply. A fly landed on the horse closest to her. A rippling tremor moved over his flank. A second fly joined it. The animal stomped anxiously at the ground. Many considered docking an elegant tradition, but how was a horse supposed to flick away flies with their stubby tails? It was quite absurd.

Mr. Williams gave his driver their destination and turned his attention back to Mara.

"After you, my dear." He opened the buggy door, placing his hand firmly under her elbow, guiding her towards the seat. Once inside, she felt uncomfortable by his attentiveness.

He watched her until she turned away, looking at the street.

"Do you enjoy living in San Francisco?" she asked, hoping to re-direct his attention.

"Call me James, please," he answered. He stared at Mara without blinking. "And yes, I find this town…quite interesting." He spoke as if his mind were elsewhere.

"Ah, here we are." The carriage pulled up alongside an empty building, old newspapers covered a large front window.

They climbed out of the passenger seats. Mara was relieved to have her personal space again, but the moment was cut short as he took her arm in his, "Well young lady, let's take a look, shall we?"

Mara forced a smile, and yet she was becoming increasingly uneasy by Mr. Williams' forwardness.

He took a key out from his vest pocket and they made their way inside. The air inside was stuffy, a lingering aroma of mold and dust.

"Well, as I've said, it needs some work."

Mara looked around the spacious building. It was definitely big enough for a gallery, and the windows would bring in natural light. Though as her eyes wandered, she saw the watermarks on the ceiling, the peeling wallpaper, and cracks in the hardwood floors.

"Mr. Williams, what was your monthly rate again?"

"Well, if you agree to take care of the appropriate repairs, twenty five dollars a month should suffice."

Mara breathed in deeply. If this were a bargain she surely would have trouble paying more for another property. She exhaled slowly. Feeling somewhat trapped, she answered, "Alright, I'd like to lease your property."

He looked at her as a hunter might looks at his prey. "Wise choice, wise choice, indeed."

As they rode back to the bank, Mara's mind raced. A sick feeling washed over her. She became lost in her thoughts. Back in the office, Mr. Cohen prepared the necessary paperwork. When it was finished, he stood up, gathering his gloves and hat, "I'm looking forward to doing business with you, Miss McClain. Rent is due at the first of the month. Penalties are applied to late payments." A smile flickered, but was gone when he made his way to the door. "Good afternoon."

Mara was relieved when he'd left.

"The bank closes early on Friday. I'm picking up Miss Lowe on the way home. Can I offer you a ride?" Mr. Cohen asked.

"Oh, thank you very much."

On the way home, the group took turns discussing Mara's new business arrangement. She was quiet during most of the conversation. Betty noticed, and looked over at her with concern. Once they were back at the house, the women made their way to their rooms. At the top of the stairs, Miss Lowe placed her hand on Mara's shoulder. "Everything all right?" she asked.

Mara was surprised at her intuition. "I'm fine. It's probably just a bad case of nerves."

"Something's bothering you."

"Well…" she hesitated "It's Mr. Williams. He gives me a…funny feeling. There's something about his eyes—they're very strange. It's like he's looking right through me. I'm sure it sounds crazy."

"No, it doesn't. Do you really want to go through with this?"

"I don't see any other option. I can barely afford this property. Anything more would wipe out my savings."

"I might be able to move some things around in my shop. Perhaps you could sell some paintings in my store?"

Mara was touched by the offer.

"That's kind of you. I'm grateful, but, I need to do this on my own. And I already signed the contract," she sighed

"All right, but be careful, please. I don't like the sound of this man."

"I will. I just need to get my business off the ground, and to pay the rent on time. I'll be fine," she said trying to sound confident. She smiled at Betty and turned down the hall on her way to her room. With the door closed, she took off her shoes and sat down on the edge of the bed. The entire afternoon seemed like a dream. She tried to tell herself it'd be all right. That it'd all work out. She stretched out on top of the lavender comforter, desperately in need of a nap. When she closed her eyes, she saw Mr. Williams's strange eyes staring back. They were cold and dark. She turned on her right side, anticipating the peace of an afternoon nap. Sleep came quickly, though the dreams that followed were not so comforting.

* * * *

A bride ran through a crimson forest. Auburn curls fell around her face and shoulders. Her bare feet were bloodied and bruised.

Mara watched in silence. Why was she running? A feeling of doom fell over her and she sensed the young woman's terror. She shadowed her in the fading light.

Her heart raced in her chest. The heavy gown snagged the ground with each painful step. The sharp cries of ravens echoed in the distance, their shrill voices lamenting the approaching twilight. Jagged stones protruded along the trail. Her bare feet suffered from the brutal terrain. Rich soil began to take on a sandy texture as she neared the shoreline. Daylight faded and washed shadows over the landscape. If she could only find her way back to the safety of the main road, back to the village of Kinvara. The aroma of the sea was rich and intoxicating. Woodlands quickly gave way to an open shore. Dark waters raged and heaved against the rising tide. Rock cliffs surrounded her on both sides. She had followed the wrong path.

The icy water rolled toward her as she slowed at the sandy bank. With resignation, she watched the churning waves of Galway Bay. Dunguaire Castle appeared like a phantom beacon through the foggy haze; dim lights glowed in the windows of the grand building. Cold ripples drifted over her battered feet. The water was salty and harsh on her open wounds. Taking a deep breath, embracing the pain, she made the sign of the cross and whispered a silent prayer to Jesus and the Mother Mary. Heavy footsteps made their way toward her. Inhaling the aroma of the overlapping waves calmed her mind. He stood behind her in silence. The young woman held her ground. Rough hands encircled her delicate neck. Her locket ripped from her throat as she was pulled under the frigid water. It floated away on the currents. Her last thoughts were of Daniel.

Chapter 8

Mara awoke with a jolt. Her face flushed, heart pounding. She sat up, looking around the room groggily. *It was a nightmare, a dream.* Darkness had settled into the room with sunset approaching. She climbed out of bed, making her way to the window. She slid open the glass and peeked outside. Crimson streaks stretched out like fingers around a swollen harvest moon. Boys were lighting street lamps below. She'd overslept. She went over to the basin and washed her face in the cool water. Droplets trickled down softly into the porcelain bowl. Autumn light mirrored in the reflective surface. After she'd freshened up, she made her way to the dining room. The aroma of fresh cooking wafted in from the kitchen. This time, she had arrived before everyone was seated. She noticed a fresh white tablecloth covering the oak dining set. Mrs. Levy was busy putting the finishing touches on the evening's supper.

"Can I help you with anything, Sarah?"

"That's very thoughtful. I could use a hand cutting up the herbs if you don't mind."

She made her way to the counter and began chopping clumps of parsley and basil.

"We're having Shabbat dinner tonight. You know what that is? Shabbat?"

"Why, no."

"I make a point of honoring the various customs and traditions of my guests. I offer special holiday meals for Christmas and Easter. And on the Sabbath and Jewish holidays, I prepare my own favorite dishes to celebrate."

"That sounds lovely, but I'm afraid I'm not familiar with…Shabbat."

"In practicing Judaism, we celebrate the Sabbath, beginning Friday at sundown and ending Saturday evening with the appearance of three stars. We refrain from work, much like Christians on Sundays. This is in honor of the Lord's creating the heavens and earth in six days, and then resting on the seventh. It's one of the Ten Commandments—to hold the

Sabbath day holy. My family enjoys preparing a special dinner, lighting candles, reciting prayers on Fridays at sundown. We call this Shabbat.

"Joshua Cohen will be leading the prayers tonight." Sarah added smiling. "He's very familiar with Shabbat dinner, as he and his family happen to be practicing Jews."

"Well, I'm very honored to be participating. Thank you."

Betty Lowe joined them in the kitchen, and they took turns bringing the dishes to the table. The evening's guests trickled into the dining room, with the exception of Jane Darby.

Betty whispered in Mara's ear, "Miss Darby never attends Shabbat dinner. Says it goes against her Baptist beliefs," she said, rolling her eyes.

Mara shook her head, and her dislike for the girl continued to grow.

Mrs. Levy stood at the head of the table and smiled. She proceeded and lit two candles, and then she covered her eyes with her hands and was quiet for a moment. Gently, she waved her hands over the open flame, directing the light toward her face.

She prayed. Afterwards, she uncovered her eyes and looked out at her guests.

Together they answered, "Shabbot Shalom."

Betty turned to Mara and explained, "Now, we greet each other and give welcome."

Around the table, people shook hands, some embraced. Patrick turned to Mara and raised her hand to his lips. He held her eyes as his mouth gently brushed the back of her skin. A tingling sensation moved over her body. Mara's heart raced in anticipation. She was vaguely aware that Sarah was speaking.

"You may all take your seats now," Mrs. Levy instructed.

Mr. Cohen made his way to the head of the table. A dark Yamaka rested atop his golden curls. As Mara looked around the table, she noticed the other men wore them as well. His song started out in Hebrew, followed by an English translation. He sang in a deep baritone.

"Come out my Beloved, the Bride to meet;
The inner light of Shabbat, let us greet.

Come out my Beloved, the Bride to meet;
The inner light of Shabbat, let us greet.
"Observe" and "Remember" in a single word,
He caused us to hear, the One and Only Lord.
G-d is One and His Name is One,
For renown, for glory and in song.
Come out my Beloved, the Bride to meet;
The inner light of Shabbat, let us greet.
To welcome the Shabbat, let us progress,
For that is the source, from which to bless.
From the beginning, chosen before time,
Last in deed, but in thought-prime.
Come out my Beloved, the Bride to meet;
The inner light of Shabbat, let us greet…"

Betty whispered into Mara's ear, "Lekhah Dodi means come my beloved. It's an appeal for a mystical "beloved" that could mean either God or one's friends to join together in welcoming Shabbat."

On the last verse, the guests were motioned to stand and look in the direction of the open door, greeting Queen Shabbat as she arrived.

After this, they took their seats, and everyone received a goblet of wine. Mrs. Levy's grandson came forward. His dark blue eyes darting around the room nervously. His hands shook as he lifted a crystal carafe. His grandmother smiled at him reassuringly. He took a deep breath and began to sing.

> *Praise to you, Adonai our God, Sovereign of the universe,*
> *Creator of the fruit of the vine.*
> *Praise to You, Adonai our God, Sovereign of the universe*
> *who finding favor with us, sanctified us with mitzvot.*
> *In love and favor, You made the holy Shabbat our heritage*
> *as a reminder of the work of Creation.*
> *As first among our sacred days, it recall the Exodus from*
Egypt.

You chose us and set us apart from the peoples.
In love and favor You have given us Your holy Shabbat as
an inheritance.

After the blessing, the group was led to the kitchen, where they took turns washing their hands. Afterwards, they sat back down at the table in silence.

Mrs. Levy uncovered two challahs. Jeremiah stepped forward and blessed the bread.

A piece of challah was placed on each plate. Once everyone was served, they began talking amongst themselves.

Joshua Cohen stood up and raised his glass. "I'd like to make a toast to Miss McClain. Congratulations on leasing the new property for your gallery. It's quite an accomplishment, and on her first day in the city no less. Mazel tov!"

"Mazel tov!" The guests chimed in. The clinking of glasses chimed throughout the room.

"Thank you, Mr. Cohen. It's been quite a day. I really appreciated your help at the bank. And I'd like to say…your opening prayer was quite moving. Mazel tov!"

"You're very welcome, dear. And I'm happy that you're celebrating Shabbat with us."

Patrick turned to Mara and leaned forward. "Joshua filled me in on your gallery needing some repairs. I'd be happy to help with that…if you're interested."

Mara smiled. "That'd be wonderful."

"If you have some time tomorrow, perhaps we could discuss it over dinner. There's a wonderful restaurant down on Dupont Street. I happen to be friends with the owners."

Mara's heart skipped a beat. Was this really happening? She tried to keep her voice steady as she answered. "Yes, Mr. Deane. I would enjoy that very much."

Betty caught Mara's gaze, smiled, and then looked down at her plate. Mara's mind was racing throughout supper. Everything was happening so quickly. She wondered how it would all end. When dinner was finished, guests took turns bringing their plates to the kitchen. After the cleanup, Betty led Mara into the parlor and they sat down in front of the fireplace

"Mara, are you excited about your dinner date with Mr. Deane?"

"Well, I don't think it's actually a date. It's really just a business meeting to discuss his work at the gallery." She tried her best to hide her growing excitement.

Betty smiled knowingly. "All right, but could you tell me how your business arrangement works out." She giggled.

"I will. It'll be nice to try one of the restaurants in town. Mr. Deane mentioned that we'd be dining on Dupont Street."

"Oh, interesting. That's in the middle of Chinatown."

"Chinatown?"

"Yes, I'm sure it will be fascinating to visit."

"I'm sure it will be. I can't wait."

They chatted for a while before saying goodnight. Mara tossed and turned for over an hour. The rhythmic sounds of hoof beats eventually lulled her into a dreamless sleep.

Chapter 9

The next day was pleasantly mild, the fog burning off early. Mara hurried through her morning routine, anxious to start her day. After breakfast, she made her way outside and walked down to the mercantile store. She'd made an early start, and there were few pedestrians outside. At the end of the street, she noticed a large sign that read, *Becker and Smith Mercantile.*

She opened the door and went in. Banging and hammering echoed from the upstairs living quarters. Jeremiah Smith was helping an elderly woman at the front counter. Mara looked around the shop, admiring their goods. Fresh produce, canned foods, and bakery items were available near the checkout. The opposite side had a variety of kitchen gadgets, cutlery sets and dinnerware. A large china cabinet held crystal goblets and dishes. Porcelain dolls hung in rows over glass shelves. She walked to the back, passing an aisle of stacked canned goods. A clothing boutique displayed a variety of dresses and stacks of colorful material, and then a small table caught her eye. An assortment of hair accessories and brushes were neatly arranged. A small butterfly comb grabbed her attention. She admired the sapphire wings flecked with pearl accents. Mara reached for it, holding it up to the light. It was soft, delicate, and would go perfectly with her favorite blue dress. She bit down on her lower lip, trying to decide if she dared spend the money. *Perhaps just this once.*

Mr. Smith walked up and stood beside her. "Miss McClain, what a pleasure! Welcome to our store. I see you've found something to your liking." He smiled.

"Yes, it's beautiful. I really shouldn't spend the money, but I don't think I can help myself."

"Well, dear, we all need to treat ourselves now and again. And the comb will simply look gorgeous with your blue eyes."

"Thank you, you're very kind. Well, I guess I should take a look at what I came here for, before I get tempted again. You mentioned you sell art supplies?"

He brushed the wavy locks from his forehead, studying her with a glimmer of amusement.

"I…was just about to look at some of Mr. Becker's paintings," she said, trying to sound casual.

"Please do. I'm going downstairs for a break, and I'm looking forward to dinner tonight. Mrs. Levy is letting us borrow the surrey. Six o'clock work for you?"

"Yes, that'd be very nice. Thank you."

"Perfect, I'll see you this evening, Miss McClain." His smile exposed his dimples, and he reached for his shirt, covering back up before heading downstairs. Mr. Becker led her to a large bedroom. He went to the back closet and returned with three paintings.

Mara studied the images. Together they were a triptych, a panoramic scene of the Waterfront. She admired the imagery of the Embarcadero train station, the somber horse-drawn carriages, the churning waters of the San Francisco Bay, shimmering in the fading light.

She was impressed, believing the oil paintings to be quite good, especially for a novice. The setting sun mirrored the overlapping waves, the play of light and dark breathtaking.

"They're wonderful! Would you be interested in finding a buyer for your work?"

For a moment, he could only stare, his mouth hanging open. Mara tried not to giggle at his expression. "Do you really think someone might be interested in purchasing one?"

"Why, yes, I do. I think the set is rather lovely. If you'd be interested, I would be happy to display them in my gallery. They could be on commission. When they sell, we'll both profit," she said.

"Oh, yes, Miss McClain, yes!" He clapped his hands together, spinning around in a graceful circle. "This is an absolute dream come true!"

"Well, you've just become my first featured artist! I'm absolutely thrilled, and please call me Mara," she smiled.

"Oh, yes, Mara, and of course; call me Donald. Let's go tell Jerry. He'll be so happy!" He reached for her hand and together they hurried downstairs to tell Jeremiah about the news.

Mr. Smith beamed, his eyes glistening. "Congratulations, Donald. I've always told you your paintings should be in a gallery."

"Thank you, Jerry. It means a lot." He smiled and said, "Donald, those art supplies in the corner need to be delivered to Miss McClain's new gallery. I have the key and address for you."

"I'll take them over now. Just let me know when you're ready for my paintings and I'll bring them by your new shop!"

"Wonderful."

He gathered the supplies and went back and forth from his cart, loading them carefully into the wagon. On the last trip outside, Donald appeared to float out the door, joy lighting up his face.

Mr. Smith turned to Mara. "I can't thank you enough. You just made his dream come true."

"Mr. Smith, the pleasure is all mine. Donald is quite the artist."

"Please call me Jeremiah."

"Will do, and you can call me Mara."

"Thank you, Mara. Can I tell you a little secret?"

"Absolutely."

"Donald thinks we're remodeling the upstairs to put in a sitting area. Really, it's going to be his new art studio. It's a special birthday gift that I'm giving him…" he trailed off suddenly uncertain if he'd revealed too much.

Mara smiled reassuringly, understanding that they were not only business associates, but also lovers. She realized that this might be a bit shocking for some, but it wasn't the first time she knew men that romantically loved one another. Two of her closest friends, Jason and Robert, had dated in secret during college. It didn't bother her then, and it doesn't bother her now. Love was love in her eyes.

"Your secret is safe with me! What a thoughtful gift. I know he'll be absolutely thrilled."

"Thank you, Mara," he answered with relief. "Please let us know if there's anything we can do to help with your new gallery. We can't wait!"

"I definitely will! And thank you again for my beautiful butterfly comb." She reached up and gave Jeremiah a quick peck on the cheek. I really am feeling at home."

"San Francisco is lucky to have you."

She made her way back to the boarding house with her parcel of paints and brushes. Betty was sitting in front of the fireplace with a book. She looked up when Mara entered into the room.

"I was just thinking about you. I had an idea for your gallery this morning."

"Oh, really?"

"I may have figured out a way to get some paintings for the grand opening. Maybe you could write an advertisement and place it in the local newspaper? That way, people will know that you're looking for art works for your new business. It could also stir up some excitement regarding the gallery."

"Betty, that's brilliant. I should have thought of this before. Thank you."

"You looked so happy when you came in. Having a good day?"

"I just came back from *The Smith and Becker Mercantile*. I took a look at Mr. Becker's paintings. They're actually quite wonderful. He's going to let me commission them for the gallery. I have my first triptych! I'll also have a few pieces of my own to sell. They're smaller works. I had to leave my larger canvases back home in Philadelphia, but it's a beginning."

"It sure is. Congratulations."

"Are you excited about your dinner date with Mr. Deane tonight?"

"I am, I guess. I mean, I'm a little nervous. It's not really a date…just a business meeting."

Betty nodded. "Well, your new business partner couldn't keep his eyes off of you at dinner last night," she giggled.

"Really?"

"Yes, really. I can't wait to hear how it goes."

"Thank you. Actually, I picked up a little accessory for my dress tonight." She reached down into the package, retrieving the butterfly comb.

"Oh, Mara, that's gorgeous. The color matches your eyes."

"Thank you. I think I might go upstairs and work on the

advertisement for the newspaper. Your idea was brilliant."

"Good luck."

Mara headed back to her bedroom to get to work. She brought a notebook and pen and ink set, and placed them on the desk by the window. She worked for several hours, trying to find the right words. Crumpled papers floated over the desk, and around the floor at her feet. She finished just as the sun was setting.

Realizing she'd lost track of time, she went to the wardrobe and retrieved a royal blue dress. She changed and sat down in front of the vanity, brushing her thick strawberry blond curls, and then holding them in place with the new butterfly comb. She studied her reflection in the mirror—her eyes sparkling with excitement, a rosy blush highlighting her cheekbones. Her heart raced as she made her way down the stairs, but her happiness was cut short when she recognized that one of the guests in the parlor was Jane Darby. She was sitting close to Patrick on the loveseat; her head tossed back laughing, her hand caressing his shoulder.

Mr. Deane rose to his feet as Mara entered the room. His eyes widened, as he gazed in stunned disbelief. For the first time since she'd met the man, he was speechless.

"Miss McClain, you look…breathtaking," he whispered.

From the corner of her eye, Mara glimpsed Jane Darby seething. Her lips parted, but she was unable to speak.

"Are you ready, dear?" Patrick offered his arm and led her outside. Jane rushed to the open window and watched with clenched fists, fingernails sinking deep into her palms

Patrick helped Mara into the surrey. He climbed up beside her, giving a gentle flick of the reins. They drove down the darkening street. The rustling wind scattered the ends of his hair over his face. He pushed them away absently with the back of his hand. She breathed in the aroma of chimney smoke and soft cologne. Autumn leaves blew across the cobblestones, dancing chaotic circles through shadows, the sky glowing like burning embers.

They were both quiet for the first few moments of the ride, stealing glances and smiling shyly as they made their way across Market Street toward Mission. Mara noticed a large cathedral rising toward the heavens, a Gothic silhouette shadowed by the setting sun.

"Mr. Deane, is that a Catholic Cathedral?"

"Yes, it is. That's Saint Patrick's."

"It looks lovely. I was hoping to find a nice church for Sunday Mass."

"Well, I'm sure Miss Lowe would be happy to join you. She goes every Sunday."

"Oh, really?"

"So, another Catholic girl has moved into the Levy Boarding House." He chuckled. "It appears that I had to travel all the way to America before finding my perfect Irish rose," he said quietly, his mouth pulling up in a lopsided grin. Reluctantly, he turned his attention back to the road, and turned down the block. Mara took the opportunity to drink in his features, admiring his rugged jawline, high cheekbones, charming snub nose and smoldering eyes. *No wonder Jane Darby couldn't keep her hands off him.*

The scenery changed abruptly and they found themselves in a completely foreign world. The street signs were written in Chinese. Lanterns hung along and over-top the busy avenue, swinging in the breeze like colorful paper moons. Soft lights illuminated the frenzied neighborhood. The night was loud with the hard edges of Cantonese. There was an urgency in the crowd, as if these people were racing against time. Hundreds of Chinese residents hurried over the sidewalks, some peddling bicycles. Most of the pedestrians were men. They wore long braided queues down the backs of loose fitting shirts. Mara noticed only a handful of women outside. They wore colorful silk dresses that hugged their petite figures. Several Laundromats displayed starched clothing hanging in their windows. Produce stands sold exotic fruits and vegetables. Large yellow banners advertised mysterious businesses with cloudy windows. Mara tried to make sense of the signs.

She noticed a group of men gathered outside a dark building with heavy red doors. They were bunched up in tight circles, a few of them pacing around anxiously. Smoke spilled out from an open window. The doors parted slowly, revealing a young woman in her late teens. A hazy light revealed her silhouette. She wore a bright red Quipao covered in tiny gold flowers. She smiled demurely as the gentlemen entered. These scenes repeated themselves for several blocks until they had at last reached their destination.

Mr. Deane stopped the surrey in front of a small building, *The Golden Dragon.* He helped Mara climb down and escorted her inside. It was a small restaurant, full of people, laughter, and the scents of eastern cooking. A young man made his way over to greet them.

His ebony hair was braided in a long queue. When he smiled, his face lit up like the lanterns above their heads.

"Patrick! It's wonderful to see you!"

"Miss McClain, I'd like to meet my friend, Junjie Lee. His parents own this restaurant."

"It's a pleasure to meet you, Miss McClain," he answered politely.

"Thank you, Mr. Lee. The pleasure's mine."

Mara soon realized that they were the only people speaking English. Some of the diners were taking turns staring at them. She didn't mind. It thrilled her to be able to travel just a few blocks and emerge into this magical world. It was quite the adventure.

They were escorted to a private table in the back and handed two menus. Chinese characters covered the pages.

Mr. Lee described some of the dishes listed, pointing to a few vegetarian options.

She turned to Mr. Deane. "What do you recommend?"

He thought for a moment and said, "Junjie, could we have two vegetable chow mien platters with bean curd and a bottle of plum wine?"

"Nice choice," he smiled, collecting their menus and heading back to the kitchen.

The food arrived quickly, two steaming bowls of noodles, bean curd and vegetables covered in a dark brown sauce. The aroma was tantalizing and Mara's stomach rumbled with hunger. She looked down at the chopsticks with a curious expression.

"Shall I help you with those?" Patrick asked standing up.

"Thank you."

He smiled, walked over to her chair, leaning toward her shoulder, and gently placed her fingers around the chopsticks. His hand folded over hers, guiding them through the noodles. A few moments passed, which seemed like a lifetime, before she had the hang of it. As he leaned in closer, she could feel the coarseness of his skin against her cheek. She breathed in the subtle aroma of his aftershave, the touch of his hand sending shivers down her back, as she struggled to focus. Once it appeared that Mara had mastered the use of her chopsticks, he went back to his seat and filled her glass with plum wine. She took a sip; the rich beverage rolled down her throat, warming her belly. She felt at ease and wanted the night to go on forever. Meanwhile, she tried her best to gather the slippery noodles up with the slender pieces of wood. When she had finally managed to wrestle a hunk of chow mien between the sticks, just inches from her lips, the points crossed and the noodles slipped and fell onto her lap. She looked up, embarrassed, but caught the glimmer in Patrick's eyes, and they laughed until tears welled in their eyes. When they'd composed themselves, Patrick leaned back in his chair, took a sip of his wine, and steadied her with a thoughtful look.

"I'm really looking forward to working for you over the next few weeks."

"I am, too," she said smiling. "But I should probably ask you how much you charge before you start to work. I'll make sure to have your money ready by Monday."

His eyes flickered for a moment.

"Well, I had an idea about that." He took a sip of wine before going on. "I was thinking we might do an exchange."

"An exchange?" Mara asked, raising her brow.

"I'd like to ask you a favor. You see…it's not everyday that I get the chance to work for a lovely young artist. I was wondering if we might exchange my labor for one of your paintings?"

"Really? What'd did you have in mind?"

"Well, I hope you don't think it's strange…but I'm quite fond of my old horse, Sammy, and I'm afraid he's getting a little long in the tooth. That old boy means the world to me. I don't know how many more winters we'll be sharing, and so it might be nice to have a painting done of him before he passes on." His eyes glazed over, and he blinked, looking towards the open window.

Mara was touched.

"I'd be more than happy to paint Sammy. I'd consider it an honor, but is that enough for all the labor you'll be doing at the shop? I know it'll be taking you away from your other jobs."

"No, dear, it's more than enough, and I'm going to be boxing in some matches over the next couple of weeks in the evenings. I'll be earning my keep that way," he said with a far off look.

Mara was quiet, fretting over the possibility of him being injured.

As if reading her thoughts, he asked, "Is everything alright?"

She collected herself and tried to smile. "Oh yes…I think it's a lovely idea. Perhaps you'd like to pose with Sammy?"

His eyes widened. "Oh? Well…I never really considered it…but it would be interesting, I suppose."

"Perhaps you could take a few work breaks during the day. There's a paddock behind my new gallery. I could set up my easel and paint the both of you."

Patrick was quiet for a moment, studying his glass. "I think that'd be just fine." They smiled at one another, comfortable in their silence, the cool wine easing their nerves.

"Oh, I did have an idea for your gallery before I forget. Junjie happens to be an accomplished artist himself. His parents came to San Francisco during the height of the Gold Rush. They moved from Beijing, China. He's spent his entire life in San Francisco, which is why his English is so excellent. We've been on a few carpentry jobs together. He's actually going to be taking over at the mercantile store for the next few weeks, but he paints in his spare time. His work deals a lot with Chinese heritage. Think you might be interested in taking a look at some of his paintings?"

"Absolutely."

After paying for their meal, Patrick helped Mara out of her seat, taking her by the arm towards the upstairs living quarters. Junjie turned around by the front entrance, paused nervously, and asked if they wouldn't mind taking off their shoes before entering, and so they took turns stripping off their footwear.

"Miss Mara, this is my mother and father, Mr. and Mrs. Lee."

His parents were sitting in the dining room finishing supper. They seemed surprised by the unexpected guests, but smiled warmly all the same. Junjie explained that they both spoke little English. His mother stood up from the table, a petite woman with delicate features, and motioned for them to take a seat. Within moments, there was hot tea and sugar cakes. Mr. And Mrs. Lee studied them with curious expressions, smiling while the young couple thanked them for their dessert and drinks. Mara looked around the room, sipping her tea, admiring the colorful decorations and the otherwise modest home. There were several jade animal figurines along the shelves. Family photographs covered the walls, a few scenes from China.

The logs in the fireplace crackled; a golden Buddha rested on its hearth. A dish of fresh oranges was set to the left, burning sticks of incense to the right. The ends glowed red with spiraling smoke that floated lazily towards the ceiling.

Junjie came back into the room carrying five large paintings. He propped them up alongside the fireplace. Each canvas depicted a different animal. The largest work was of a dragon rising from the sea, its golden scales glittering in the soft light.

"In our culture, our birth years are represented by the Zodiac. So, if you were born in 1849, you'd be the *Year of the Monkey*." He lifted one of the paintings, a brown monkey with expressive eyes grasping the branches of a tree. The hair appeared to shimmer with flakes of gold.

"Miss Mara, may I ask your birth year?"

"Why, yes, it's 1848."

"Ah, the *Year of the Horse*. A very good animal."

He held up a painting of a golden horse running through a green field flecked with white lilies and yellow daffodils.

"That's stunning!"

"Thank you. People born during the *Year of the Horse* are said to be kind, sentimental and straightforward. And you, Patrick?"

"Oh, me? 1845."

He smiled, reaching for one of the paintings. *"Year of the Tiger."* As he held up the image, she noticed that the orange and black fur was highlighted by what appeared to be gold dust. The style was unique—realistic imagery, but with broken brush strokes. It reminded her of the photograph that Betty had shown her of Monet's haystacks. The paintings had an electric quality to them, giving the animals the appearance of being in motion.

"People born in the *Year of the Tiger* are said to be brave, confident, and adventurous. The horse and tiger are romantically compatible," Junjie replied with a smile. Patrick gave Mara a quick wink. She smiled back, studying the image with fascination.

"Your paintings are lovely, so…original. You know, I'm looking for pieces for my gallery. What would you think about showing your work in my studio? I'm planning on having a grand opening soon. I'd love to have your canvases on display."

"Yes, I'd like that very much. Thank you."

They discussed the details of commissioning the pieces and arranged a day to drop off the artworks. Afterwards, they said their goodbyes and headed back to the surrey. The night was cold and dark, the fog pressing down on the city. The street lamps glowed eerily in the haze. Mara winced as the wind whipped past, her body shivering in the breeze. Patrick reached his arm around her waist and scooted her closer. They smiled at one another as they rode along. Once they were back at the house, Mara offered to help Patrick with the horses. He was patient and showed her how to safely remove the tack and reins, and then how to hang them on the paddock wall. When they were finished, the horses settled in their stalls. They stood silently together in the soft light of the barn. Patrick leaned toward Mara, gently taking her hands in his, their eyes locking. His lips brushed against her eager mouth, warm and tender. His strong arms embraced her, pulling her close, and for a moment, it seemed like they were one person, melting against one another, floating through time and space.

Slowly their eyes opened, hearts drumming with desire. Patrick smiled down at her flushed face.

"I better get you inside. I can't have my little Irish rose shivering in the cold." He gave her a quick peck on the nose and escorted her back to the house. They walked up the stairs hand in hand.

"Good night, darlin'." They kissed goodbye outside her bedroom.

The door closed behind her. Mara could barely contain her excitement. She paced back and forth, trying to release her pent-up energy. It would be hard to sleep tonight. She undressed in a happy daze, snuggled under the covers, and clicked open her diary.

Mara and Patrick were oblivious to the fact someone had been watching from down the hall. Jane Darby clenched her jaw, spying through a small opening in her bedroom door. When they were both back in their rooms, she quietly closed the wooden barrier and threw herself on top of the bed. The tears she cried were not tears of sorrow. No, they were tears of rage.

* * * *

Mrs. Levy's table was full for Sunday breakfast, the guests quietly helping themselves to generous helpings of French toast, scrambled eggs and fresh fruit. Mara and Patrick occasionally stole glances at one another, happy in their blossoming romance.

Joshua looked over at Mara and said, "Betty said you might want to attend church this morning. Could I give you two a ride?"

"Yes, thank you. That's very thoughtful."

Jane stared for a moment and then asked, "Is it true what they say about Catholics?"

Mara turned and looked at the girl. She tried to keep her voice calm as she spoke. "What is it that they say?"

"That Catholics worship statues in their churches." She giggled. "And that ya'll practice a bunch of strange rituals," she said rolling her eyes.

"No, we don't," Mara said flatly, trying her best to love her neighbor, though failing miserably. "We're not idolatrous. The statues remind of us what we love most, Jesus, Mary, and all the saints and apostles, but we aren't worshipping the statues. That's just silly."

Jane eyed her distastefully and refused to speak to her through the remainder of breakfast. Mara caught Betty's eyes and tried not to laugh.

After breakfast, Patrick led Mara over to the parlor.

"I'm going to be gone most of the day and night. I have some sparring practice this morning, and a fight later this evening, but if things work out the way I hope, I'll have more than enough money for my new business."

"Oh, really? What kind of business?" Mara's face lit up.

"Jenjie and I have been saving our money so we can invest in a few properties. There are some really interesting homes being built over in Pacific Heights. We've been calling them *Painted Ladies*. They're pretty spectacular, architecturally speaking. The paint colors are often bold and theatrical. We have plans to build one of our own, but we need to get the capital. There's still a bit of real estate available to lease on that side of town. I just need to score a few more fights downtown. There's a big one coming up. It's quite the payday for whoever comes out on top. I know I can do it, Mara. I've got to do it. I can't go on forever like this, just scraping by, hoping to grab whatever job happens to come my way." His face grew solemn.

Mara looked down at his hands. She traced her fingers over his clenched fists. She thought of how they were strong, and yet seemed so very gentle.

"What if you get injured…or what if…" She couldn't finish as her stomach began to turn.

"I'll be fine, darlin'," he said, trying to ease her worries. "If I plan this just right, my boxing days will soon be a thing of the past. You'll see, then I'll be able to focus on what really matters." Patrick looked deep into her eyes, and she felt as if she were falling. He bent down, kissing her softly on the mouth.

They pulled apart as they heard footsteps approaching.

"Sorry to interrupt, we were just about to drive over to Saint Patrick's, if you're ready."

"Yes. Thank you."

They said their goodbyes and headed to church. A heavy weight settled in her stomach as they drove along. She tried to pay attention to the conversation, but her mind kept wandering. Before she knew it, they'd arrived at Saint Patrick's. The gothic cathedral, with its spiraling arches which faded into the clouds. A number of painted glass windows were set deeply in the stones. Betty and Mara walked up the steps and entered the dark building. They genuflected and made their way down the pew. The aroma of candles eased her mind. Mara closed her eyes and was carried along in prayer, and a feeling of contentment washed over her.

For a moment she was somewhere else, a beautiful parlor, surrounded by prisms of light. Autumn colors shone through the stained glass, dancing crystals flickered along the walls. The warm rays fell against her skin and settled on her swelling waist. She looked down toward her belly, a feeling of love so powerful that it nearly swept her away. Her hand reached down, caressing the slight bump, for a moment she could almost hear its heartbeat.

Betty placed her hand on Mara's shoulder, motioning her to stand. The congregation was rising as the church procession made its way down the aisle. Mara quickly stood to sing aloud with her neighbors. It was a beautiful Mass, led by an elderly priest with a gentle voice and an aura of kindness. His Homily was inspiring. He spoke of forgiveness and Christ's great mercy, but her mind kept drifting back to the image of the parlor, and the dancing lights. After Communion, Mara quietly prayed for her departed parents, her new friends at the boarding house, and that Patrick would be safe during his boxing matches. She also said a small prayer for herself, that she might overcome the challenges of her new life.

Outside the church, Mara and Betty chatted while they waited for Joshua Cohen to drive them home.

"Did you have a nice dinner with Mr. Deane last night?"

"Very nice," she said, looking down at her hands. When she looked back up, Betty was grinning.

"You look so happy." She paused for a moment, her green eyes widening. "It must be such a magical thing…to have someone look at you the way he does."

"It's all so new and exciting. I've never felt this way before. It's strange but it feels like we've known each other forever, and now that we're together, I can't help but worry about him. Betty, he's boxing tonight. What if he gets hurt? I don't what I'd do if something happened to him…" her words trailed off as she looked back down at her hands.

"That must be terribly worrisome, but he's been boxing for some time now. It's not his first fight and probably won't be his last. I know it's hard, but try to have some faith. Maybe say a prayer or two." She smiled reassuringly. "Are you going to watch the fight tonight?"

"Oh, I don't think I could bear it. I didn't get much sleep last night; I was a little excited after our dinner," she said looking down the street. "I think I'm going to read my new book this afternoon and try to go to bed early."

Betty nodded and smiled. A carriage soon made its way down the quiet road, pulling up alongside them. Joshua Cohen climbed down and helped the women to their seats. Mara noticed the way Joshua occasionally stole glances at Betty during the ride back, but she seemed completely oblivious to his attention.

The three friends spent the remainder of the day in the parlor reading books. By the late afternoon, Mara's mind was flooded with images of Patrick's beaten body, surrounded by faceless strangers. She skipped dinner, turning into bed early and retrieved her rosary from the nightstand. Quietly, she recited her *Hail Mary's* and *Our Father's* praying for Patrick's safety. She slipped in and out of sleep, fitfully, never fully resting.

At midnight, she heard footsteps on the stairs. She slipped a robe over her nightgown and opened the door. Patrick moved gingerly up the steps, his eyes widening as he saw Mara at the top. She let out a gasp as a sliver of moonlight slipped over his face. Dark purple bruises covered his right eye; his bottom lip was swollen and bleeding.

"Patrick!"

He made his way over to her, trying to put on a brave face.

"Oh, no! You're hurt," she cried, her eyes traveling over his darkening bruises.

"Darlin', it's nothing. You should have seen the other guy," he whispered with a grimace. "I won the match. It's all good."

"Oh, Patrick, you poor thing." He reached down, gently pushing the loose curls from her eyes. He looked down at her hands and a smile spread over his face.

"What a good girl, sayin' your rosary before you hit the feathers. You're a sweet one, you are."

Mara noticed him wincing. "Can I help you, Patrick?"

"I'm afraid that I'm a bit of a mess."

Mara walked him back to his room. When the door was closed, her eyes darted around nervously. She had never been alone in a man's bedroom before. He smiled gently, trying to put her at ease.

"Why don't you sit there on your bed, and I'll get you some cool water." The corner of his mouth rose. "You don't' have to ask me twice." Mara's face blushed as she imagined what it would be like to join him. She busied herself with the water pitcher, wetting one of the hand towels. She carried it back along with a dry one and examined his bruises.

"The blood is seeping through your shirt."

"I guess it is," he said, looking down.

"Maybe you better take it off so I can wash off the blood."

She looked away as he pulled his shirt over his head. His chest was damp with perspiration, and flecked with streaks of blood.

"This might hurt, I'm afraid." She carefully washed his face, the cool water rolling over his bruised skin. He winced when the cloth touched his black eye, but smiled all the same.

"You have a nice touch," he said, gazing at her face. She smiled and continued to clean his wounds, her hands traveling over his muscular arms and chest. Her heart quickened with the intimacy, never having been so close to a man's bare skin.

When she was satisfied, she said, "Well, I guess I should probably get back to my room and let you get some sleep. You've had a long night, and we'll have some work tomorrow if you're up to it."

"Oh, I'm up for it," he said, his voice thick and heavy.

They looked at each other silently, hearts racing. He reached for her hands and guided them to his shoulders. His right hand gripped her waist as he lowered her onto his lap. Her robe fell open. His muscles in his thighs felt taut underneath her legs, as well as his manhood, which pressed against her, and took her breath away. He kissed her fully on the mouth, his eyes looking into hers, his lips traveling over her throat, caressing the wispy material covering her breasts. Mara lost herself in his embrace. She felt his hands gripping her shoulders, gently pushing her down onto the bed. Their chests pressed close, so new and yet strangely familiar. There was little separating them as he pulled her even closer. Her body began to awaken with an overpowering desire, and she couldn't imagine being anywhere other than his arms, in his bed, and with this, she was at peace. Her hands traveled longingly over his muscular body, they were greedy to get their fill, her mouth eagerly accepting his kisses and demanding more. And then, when she could barely contain herself, he slowly pulled back as if awakening from a dream. Patrick sat up quickly.

"I'm so sorry. I don't know what came over me," he said with a hoarse voice.

Mara's head was spinning, and she was not ready for the moment to end.

He reached for her hands and helped her to her feet.

"You're a good girl. I'm so sorry, lass. I should never have been so forward. I'm afraid I lost control…you're just so beautiful…I couldn't help myself. Please forgive me."

He looked at her with such pain and regret that Mara couldn't help but feel guilty.

"No, it's not your fault…it's mine. I'm afraid…I don't know what came over me."

Something of a smile surfaced on Patrick's face. Looking somewhat relieved, he brought her hands to his lips. I'll make sure not to take such liberties in the future. I'm so sorry, my love." He escorted her back down the hall, a bit to Mara's disappointment, and stopped at the threshold of her bedroom door.

"Goodnight, little rose. I'll see you in the morning." He gave her a small peck on the forehead before heading back down the hallway.

Mara watched with a heavy heart as he made his way into his room. The door closed with a terrible finality. It was as if miles were suddenly separating them. She felt uneasy considering her conduct, being taught at an early age that a lady should never be alone in a man's bedroom, unless of course, that man was her husband, but there was another part of her that wanted to throw those teachings out the window and discover what she'd been missing. It took a long time to fall asleep that night, tossing and turning, her body yearning for something she was only beginning to understand. When the rooster crowed outside her window, bringing the cool morning light with it, she felt reborn. She sighed deeply, stood up straight, shoulders back, and readied herself for the new day.

Chapter 10

Mara and Patrick arrived late to breakfast Monday morning. Sarah's eyes widened when she saw the bruises on his face. She took notice of the couple's nervousness and wondered if something was wrong. She'd been aware of their growing fondness for one another and hoped things would work out for them.

She turned to Patrick and said, "You're welcome to use the surrey today, since you're planning to work on the new gallery. I imagine that it might come in handy if you have to pick up some supplies."

"That's very kind, Miss Levy. My friend Junjie will be lending me a cart for the next couple of weeks, but I won't have it until tonight. So, that works out perfectly."

After breakfast, Patrick helped Mara carry her paints and supplies to the surrey. An uncomfortable silence fell over them as they drove along. Mara wished she'd never followed Patrick back to his room last night. He seemed so distant now, almost a stranger.

It was a relief when they arrived at the gallery. At least, she had something to distract her from the growing tension between them. Mara took out her key and led them inside. Patrick was quiet as he examined the peeling wallpaper, water leaks, and rotting floorboards.

"Oh, boy. Your landlord wasn't kidding when he said this property needed work. The water damage alone is going to take several days to repair."

Mara's heart sunk when she heard this. Everything seemed to be going downhill in a hurry.

"Is it too much for you," she asked, trying to hide her dismay.

"No, I can handle it, but I might need a little help with painting the walls if you don't mind."

"Of course not."

"Well then, let me head back over to the mercantile shop and pick up some supplies. Now that I've seen the damage, I have a pretty good idea what we'll need to fix it."

"Alright. Let me give you some money." Mara reached for her pocketbook and handed Patrick some coins. "Let me know if you need any more. I can go to the bank on the way home."

Patrick looked uncomfortable when he took her money, a brooding look in his eyes.

"I'll be back shortly," he said, quietly.

When he'd left, Mara walked around the room, trying to picture where she'd place the new paintings.

She was busy sorting through her art supplies and didn't hear the door open. When the footsteps approached, she looked up anticipating Patrick. Instead, Mr. Williams stood by the front entrance, gazing in her direction. His face still held the same somber expression she'd seen at the bank, but there was something different about his eyes. There was a bit of a sparkle in them, almost softness.

"Miss McClain, it's a pleasure to see you this morning. I was in the neighborhood and thought I might stop in and see how things are coming along."

Mara was disappointed to see her landlord. Although things were a bit awkward with Patrick, it was far more comfortable to be alone with him than Mr. Williams.

"What a pleasure, Mr. Williams. My friend just left to get some supplies. He's hoping to have the repairs completed within the next couple of weeks. If we're lucky, I might have my grand opening by the end of the month." She smiled, trying her best to appear confident.

"Well, that's splendid, it sounds like it's working out rather smoothly. Very good." He stared at her as if trying to memorize the details of her face. His expression was a mixture of longing and regret.

"Is everything alright?"

He was quiet for a moment, and then seemed to gather himself.

"Yes...and please call me James."

The door suddenly opened with a blast of cold air. Patrick backed inside the room with his arms full of lumber. A few fall leaves blew in from the street, scattering across the damaged floors. He carefully set the planks down, smiling, and then his expression turned to shocked disbelief.

"Patrick Deane, this is my new landlord, James Williams."

The men stood in silence, eyes locked. Mara looked back and forth between them, wondering what was the matter.

Patrick walked over and stood in front of Mara in a protective manner. "I know Mr. Williams. Yes…we met many years ago, in Kinvara."

James' mouth narrowed down into a thin line. His eyes grew dark, no longer showing any hint of softness.

"Oh, yes, I do believe I remember you. One of the Deane boys. Your family couldn't manage their farm properly, nearly lost it due to gross neglect."

Patrick's face reddened, and his eyes grew so dark that she feared for her landlord's safety, but all she could seem to do was stand there, frozen in shock.

"No, you son of a bitch, your family took advantage of a terrible situation. You enjoyed torturing the villagers with your constant pay hikes, and when that wasn't enough, you had our healthy crops shipped overseas. You knew people were starving, and you did nothing. Your family took everything, the wheat, the money, and then when there was nothing left, you kicked the farmers out of their homes, leaving the rotten potatoes in the fields. I had to move away to help pay their bills. They were starving by the time I made it to America. You turned a bad situation into a tragedy. If you hadn't sold the farm when you did, I don't know what my family would have done. The new owners were generous folks. They allowed us to share the wheat crops and vegetables while we recovered from the famine. We paid them back, with interest, and why don't you tell Miss McClain the reason that you sold your properties?" Patrick's eyes were filled with blind rage, the veins bulging out on the sides of his neck.

Mara moved between the men. She worried if Patrick didn't calm down soon, he'd wind up getting locked in a jail cell. "Please, there must be some misunderstanding."

Mr. Williams looked at Mara, put on his hat and gloves, and then walked towards the door. "I'll be checking in later to see how the repairs are going. I'll ask you to keep this peasant out of my way when I return. Good day."

He slammed the door behind him.

Patrick paced back and forth, trying to calm himself. Finally, he turned to Mara and looked down at her with such sorrow that her heart tightened.

"Please, Patrick, what's happening? I don't understand."

He suddenly swept her up in his arms, kissing her forehead and then her mouth, so urgently, and with such passion, her legs felt they might buckle.

"Mara, I can't have anything happen to you. I just can't. I've waited my entire life to find you, and I can't watch this happen again."

"What are you talking about? I don't understand."

He released her and paced back and forth, taking deep breaths to calm himself.

"Mara, you remember when I told you about growing up in a little town in Galway Ireland. In Kinvara?"

"Yes, I remember."

"Well, I didn't want to say too much about why I left…because the memories are quite disturbing."

"I've heard about the *Famine*," she said gently, taking his hand in hers.

"Yes, hearing about it and being there are two different things, my love. You see, it didn't just happen overnight. It began with the potato crops slowly failing, but not all at once. There would be talk about a neighboring farm losing some crops, and then it would start to spread. Once the blight really set in, it struck out like wildfire. Many of the villagers were tenement farmers, like my family. We relied on our potato crops as our main food supply. Our lands were divied up. Our share was quite small compared to the landlord's holdings."

"You said Mr. Williams was your landlord?"

"Yes, but there's so much more to the story. Not all of our crops failed. There were other vegetables and grains available. We had wheat growing healthy and strong on the south side of the property, but the potatoes were our main staples for cooking, especially during the winter months when the wild herbs and berries were scarce. Without them, we had trouble paying our rents, and our main food source was gone. Landowners were not happy about losing money. So, they started shipping the healthy crops over to England, sometimes America. The Williams' family was exporting every last piece of grain from their properties, including my family's farm. This left my parents and neighbors in a terrible situation. We couldn't pay our rents, so we kept getting further behind, crawling deeper into debt, until we were left with hardly any food for ourselves. The potatoes were rotting in the fields, while the healthy crops were exported overseas.

"And the potatoes could fool you. They'd look fine at first. You'd gather them up, and think you'd found some good ones, but once you cut into the flesh, a puff of pungent smoke would rise, and they'd be black as tar inside. They were completely inedible, and so people were starving to death. Children starved. My God. Pray that you never witness the pitiful sight of starving children." His eyes glassed over and he looked away.

"There were little ones walking around the village with bloated bellies, begging and crying in the streets. I was a teenager when it happened. Against my family's wishes, I stole aboard a ship one night, heading to America. The crew figured out after a few days at sea. They took mercy on me, and I was given a chance to earn my travel to America. I did all kinds of odd jobs onboard. Once we landed, I grabbed whatever work I could find. I learned carpentry skills along the way, eventually became apprenticed. And so my work helped to keep my family afloat for a while. Thankfully, another owner took possession of our land before they lost everything. This was about a year after I'd left.

"The new owners were high standing citizens in the community and quite wealthy. They bought up all of the Williams' properties when they went on the market. They were compassionate, and gave my family time to get back on their feet. We eventually managed to pay back our debts and keep the farm."

Mara's mind was racing. "But why did the Williams' family sell their land to the new owners?"

Patrick's face grew dark as he stepped closer. "Oh, Mara, that's the worst part of this story. I'm afraid to even tell you this."

"But you must."

"All right, but you have to promise me something, Mara. You must never be alone with him again."

"Why, Patrick? What are you not telling me?"

He took a deep breath and continued. "At the start of the famine, just when things were beginning to unravel, there was a young couple in town that were planning to get married. Katie and Daniel were their names. There was talk that James had his eyes set on the young girl, but she rebuffed him. On the day of their wedding," he paused, "there was a terrible accident."

"What kind of accident?" A searing pain gripped her stomach.

The bride and groom were found dead. Daniel had been shot outside the church. The bullet went right through the heart. Katie was discovered near the woods, between two cliffs at the seashore. She was face down in the water when they spotted her. The sheriff said she'd been strangled."

Mara took in a deep breath, her veins suddenly felt like they were filled with ice water. "What did she look like?"

"Why?"

"Please, just tell me."

"Alright," he said, his face bent with confusion. "Well, she was quite lovely, petite and fair like you, and she had long red curls. It's strange, but there is a resemblance between you two. I never noticed it before."

Mara sucked in her breath, and suddenly felt dizzy.

The image of the young bride running through a scarlet forest swam before her eyes. It was impossible, but somehow she knew she'd dreamed of Katie's murder. A blanket of gray clouded her vision. Mara started to swoon, and Patrick grabbed her before she hit the floor.

"Mara, are you all right," he cried, hugging her to his chest.

She opened her eyes slowly, looking around the room in confusion. "What happened?"

"I think you fainted, love. Are you alright?"

"I think so. It's just that my dream…it was so real."

"What dream, Mara?"

"I had a terrible dream the other night. There was a bride in a crimson forest. She was running for her life, and then she was pushed under the icy waves…" she trailed off, overcome with emotion. "Did they catch the murderer?"

"Let's get you some fresh air, maybe a cool drink. You look white as a ghost."

"Please just tell me! Did they catch him?"

"No, that's the thing…there were rumors."

"What kind of rumors?"

"There was a lot of talk suggesting that James had murdered the girl." Patrick's voice seemed like it was coming from a distance, a sickening feeling washed over her.

"Why wasn't he arrested?"

"That's the thing," his eyes grew dark, his fists clenched. "His family had so much power in town. There was talk, but even the sheriff was afraid to pursue it. The pressure must have finally gotten to the Williams' family, because one day they'd all disappeared along with their son. Nobody's heard from them since…not until today, that is."

"I'm going to mention this to the city's sheriff, Paul Carpenter. He's a good man, a friend of mine. I don't know if there's anything he can do about it, but at least it's a start. So listen, darlin', I mentioned earlier that I'm going to be sparring and fighting in matches for the next couple of weeks. I hope you don't mind, but I'm going to ask Jenjie to check in on you while I'm gone. He'll make sure that the landlord's not bothering you. There's a big match coming up. I just need to win a few more fights to qualify. I'll make enough money so you won't have to worry about Mr. Williams."

"But I can't ask you to do that. I couldn't take your money."

"What if it was our money?"

"What do you mean?"

With a solemn face, Patrick went down on one knee. "I wanted to do this right and with a beautiful ring…everything you deserve, but seeing that things are happening so fast, I don't want to wait. I love you, Mara. I realize that we've only known each other for just a short time, but I fell in love with you the moment I saw you in the alley, clenching your little hatpin. You're the most amazing woman I've ever met, so spirited and passionate. You're smart as a whip, too, and so very lovely. I know I don't deserve you, but I'm going to ask you anyway. Would you do me the honor of being my wife?"

Mara was overwhelmed with emotion. Tears of joy spilled down her face as she gazed into his loving eyes.

"Oh, Patrick, I love you, too. I was afraid that your feelings had changed after last night."

"Never, darlin'. I was just mad at myself for being so thoughtless. I didn't want you to imagine that I had the wrong intentions," He smiled. "I was afraid that you'd think less of me." His face suddenly lit up and he laughed, "Walking you back to your room last night was the hardest thing I've done in my life!"

"It wasn't that easy for me, either." She blushed.

His eyes glimmered when he realized the passion they shared. He drew her tight against him and looked deep into her eyes.

"So, it's a yes, my love?"

"Yes!" He picked her up as if she weighed nothing, swinging her around the room in a circle. They laughed as he twirled her around the gallery.

"I'm afraid, I don't have your ring yet, but maybe it's best we keep this to ourselves just for now," he said thoughtfully. "Maybe it should be a secret engagement until this boxing mess is over. The fighting that I'm doing doesn't always attract the most wholesome people. You see, there's a lot of gambling involved and money at stake. I'd rather not bring you into the limelight until after the fights are over. I have to keep you safe, my love, and then we can announce our engagement to the world. I'll shout it from the rooftops," he said, covering her with kisses.

Chapter 11

After holding each other for what seemed like forever, they reluctantly got back to work. Patrick busied himself repairing the walls and ceiling. It was hard labor, but he embraced it eagerly, knowing they were working together toward their future. They stole glances at one another throughout the morning. At noontime, Mara took Patrick by his hand and led him out to the paddock. Her easel was set up next to the open window. She looked for the best angle of lighting and made sure Patrick and Sammy were comfortable before going back to her canvas.

Her eyes traveled over his face and body. He looked back with a soft smile, the afternoon light shining in his dark eyes. Golden highlights radiated around his pupils. She dipped the brush into the oil paint and the droplets clung for a moment in suspended animation. A hand moved gracefully over the canvas, releasing the first colorful dot onto a sea of white. Her mind traveled to a different realm, and she joined in spirit with every human being whomever dared to take that first stroke, and she knew the risks; she was willing to pay the price, because wasn't that what the heart longed for? Whether it be by writing, painting, or music—one only needs to find the strength of courage to walk along the creative path, to search for one's higher self, and maybe, for just a moment, to gaze into the eyes of God.

While she painted his features, his essence poured out to her, and she eased every last drop onto the canvas. She channeled his spirit and bridged an even deeper sense of intimacy between them. Mara worked for over an hour in deep concentration, until they heard voices calling from outside the paddock walls. Betty and Joshua were standing on the sidewalk, a large basket set between them.

"Hi! We thought we'd drop by with some lunch. We're taking a break from work. Thought you might like to join us."

They looked at one another and smiled. "That's very thoughtful." Their friends walked around the gallery, complimenting them on their progress. Mara wanted to share the engagement news, but figured it would be best to wait. After lunch, they went back to work, and the hours flew by unnoticed. They hitched Sammy to the surrey in the fading light. Once seated, Mara leaned her head against Patrick's broad shoulder. Autumn light washed over the two lovers, painting them a golden silhouette.

* * * *

Over the next couple of weeks, Patrick and Mara kept to their daily routine. Sammy pulled their cart to and from the gallery. They worked diligently, and the building began showing improvement within the first few days. Once the walls and ceilings were repaired, Mara helped with painting. She chose a pistachio green for the accent walls, and an eggnog hue she applied to the surrounding surfaces. Their excitement grew as they finished the final restorations. Mara placed an ad in the local paper, requesting artists to drop by with their work.

Patrick continued to fight in the evenings, and his bruises advertised his winnings. There were many challenges along the way, but they worked together to try to solve them. Before long, the gallery was close to completion. On their final day of restoration, Patrick took a detour, turning towards the Pacific Heights neighborhood.

"Mara, there's a little something I want to show you." She recognized the area, as it was just a few blocks from Chinatown. They turned down a busy road, opening up to several vacant lots, but at the end of the street was a house rising from the earth. It was a grand estate, dramatic in its architectural design.

Patrick parked the cart and helped Mara climb down to the sidewalk. They watched as several men worked along the suspended scaffolding.

"This is one of those *Painted Ladies* I was telling you about. Jenjie and I are planning to start building them when we have enough money. What do you think?"

Mara looked at the building. A shower of turrets and towers rose towards the heavens. Stained glass panels were set in arched windows. The glass glittered and appeared to have been sprinkled with stardust.

"Oh, my. Can you imagine what it would be like to live in one?"

He was quiet for a moment before answering. "Could you see

yourself living in a house like this?" "Oh, yes. It's so romantic, like a fairytale. I just love it! With a bit of paint color to brighten the outside, it would be exquisite." She looked over at the trees along the sidewalk. "Like those lovely maples," she said, pointing with her gloved hand, and as she said this, the wind picked up, scattering handfuls of colorful leaves around their feet. "Yes, I think a house like this should definitely be painted with fall colors. She should be a proper autumn lady!"

"That's beautiful, Mara. Always the imaginative one," he said. "One of the many things I love about you, lass. *Autumn Lady*," he whispered.

Their peaceful musings were interrupted by high-pitched screams from down the street. Suddenly, everyone was running to see what was happening. Carriages and pedestrians blocked the road. They looked at one another alarmed, before climbing into their cart. The crowd was gathered around a horse and carriage a couple of blocks away. Women were screaming, hands covering their faces. Mara glimpsed an elderly woman making the sign of the cross.

As they got closer, Mara gasped. In the middle of the street was a deceased man lying in a pool of blood, his wagon had overturned, apparently crushing him. There were shattered wooden boxes everywhere. Bottles were rolling, the odor of whisky in the air. Looking up, Mara noticed the steep road and quickly realized that the wagon must have lost control. She wondered why the driver was transporting such a heavy load in such a small wagon. His injured horse was on the ground. Her sorrel coat was covered in blood and sweat. She labored to breathe, tongue rolling out in the dirt.

"I think that's the same cab driver that gave me a ride from The Embarcadero."

Patrick looked closer and nodded. "I believe you're right, my dear." He quickly blessed himself. "I remember the red mare. What a shame." He looked down at the bony ribcage and the track of scars along her flanks. She appeared even thinner than before.

"I wonder what happened to the black gelding." As they watched with heavy hearts, a gentleman made his way over and stood beside them. He took off his hat, and appeared to be praying.

"This is a tragedy, to be sure," he said in a deep Scottish accent.

They looked up, nodding in agreement.

"The poor creature, and just look at the ribs sticking out from under her coat. There's a better way to haul cargo around San Francisco. I've been working on some ideas in the Sacramento Valley. We've been using a pulley system for transporting freight, but I can see that something needs to be done here in San Francisco," he said passionately.

Patrick turned to him, "What do you mean, sir?"

"Let me introduce myself. The name's Andrew Hallidie. I'm an engineer by trade. I was just saying that there's better ways to get passengers and cargo up these steep hills. I've been working on something called a trolley car. It's a cable railway system. It'll take the burden off these poor animals. Horses shouldn't have to haul passengers and cargo up these dangerous hills. This new system will eventually make the horse-drawn trolleys obsolete."

"Why that's amazing, sir. I do hope you're successful," Mara said, eyes widening.

"I'll make a promise to you, lass. God willing, some day in the near future, they'll be streetcars going up and down these hills. One day you'll look out your window and see railway cars carrying passengers and cargo just like these horse-drawn carts and trolleys."

Mara smiled in wonder. A sudden movement caught her eye, and she looked back at the carriage. The mare labored to get to her feet. She struggled with her legs outstretched, straining to stand up. She managed weakly to get upright, and stood trembling in the thick fog. Mara walked over, reaching her hand up, and gently caressed the sweat-soaked coat. Although she appeared to be suffering, the mare nuzzled Mara's shoulder, letting out a contented snort. Her eyes closed while Mara continued to stroke her.

"Oh, Patrick, she's back on her feet!"

"Yes, dear, it's a good sign, but she's lost a lot of blood. I think it's going to be touch and go from here."

A few moments later, a large trailer pulled through the crowd. There were black letters written on its side reading, *San Francisco Society for the Prevention of Cruelty to Animals.*

Three men in white uniforms walked over. One circled around the mare accessing her injuries. A second placed a halter over her head. The third felt around for broken bones, seemingly satisfied, they led the horse up the ramp, and into the back of the covered trailer.

"Where are you taking her, sir?"

"We're going to have a veterinarian take a look at her injuries. If she makes it, the mare will be put up for adoption, but we'll make sure the new owner takes proper care of the poor girl. Looks like she's been through enough already."

Mara's eyes softened with relief and she looked up at Patrick. He smiled down at her and they walked back to their cart.

"Oh, I hope she makes it, Patrick, the poor thing," she sighed.

"Maybe, we should say a little prayer for her. It couldn't hurt."

They went back to the gallery to finish the final repairs. Mara was expecting visitors by Friday. She was hoping to find some suitable paintings to add to her collection. By noon, they took a break, and she worked on the finishing touches of her painting.

* * * *

Around the same time, a visitor arrived at *The Levy Boarding House.* The home was empty except for one young woman sitting alone in the parlor. Jane Darby looked out the window, hearing a loud knocking at the door.

A gentleman stood on the porch. He took off his hat as she opened the door. She noticed a streak of white cutting through his blond hair.

"Madame, I was wondering if Miss Mara McClain might be at home. I just visited the gallery and she wasn't there. I thought perhaps she might have come back to the boarding house?"

A wry smile crept over her face and she batted her eyelashes at the gentleman caller. She looked down, noticing that he was holding a box of chocolates and flowers.

Her mind began to race, and she wondered if this older man, and a rich looking one at that, might be interested in Mara. Anger burned in her chest. *Was everyone in San Francisco in love with this girl?*

"Won't you please come in? I have some information concerning Mara McClain that you may find rather interesting."

He stopped and looked at Jane Darby for a moment, his gaze traveling over her voluptuous curves.

"Alright then. I have a few minutes."

"Could I offer you some tea?"

"Yes, tea sounds lovely."

She led him back to the kitchen, smiling coyly and proceeded to serve him.

"I'm Jane Darby, and may I ask your name, sir?"

"Of course, young lady, I'm James Williams, but you can call me James, if you like," he said with a thin smile, his eyes focused on her chest.

"Mr. Williams, I hope you don't mind me mentioning that your accent is quite eloquent. I've never met anyone from…is it England?"

"Yes, it is," he replied, his eyes traveling over her figure. She smiled demurely, with an engaging tilt of the head.

After pouring his tea. She took a seat, and let out a deep sigh. "Now, I've never been one to gossip, Mr. Williams, but you seem like such a nice gentleman. I feel that's it's my Christian duty to tell you the truth."

His eyebrows rose, and he reached out and took her hand. "Dear, what's bothering your charming little head? Why don't you tell me all about it?"

She leaned back, daintily taking a sip of tea. "Well, it just so happens that Miss McClain is not a very nice young lady, no sir."

"Oh, really now. How is she not nice?" He asked with his brows knitting together, hands folded under his chin, leaning forward in his chair.

"Well, to begin with, she and that Patrick, I mean Mr. Deane, they can't seem to keep their hands off each other." Her eyes widened.

"How shocking," he said with a hint of anger in his voice.

"Why yes. I mean…I moved into this home expecting it to be a wholesome environment, a place I could relax safely while I attended school, but the things that go on in this house at night…" she said with an eye roll.

"Oh, dear, you poor girl. What kind of things are you talking about?"

"Well, just the other evening, something woke me up from a sound asleep. I was so frightened," she whimpered.

"I can imagine. How dreadful, but go on."

"I peeked out my door, and I saw Mr. Deane climbing the stairs. He was all beaten up with a black eye no less. God knows what he was up to. I've heard he boxes down on Kearny Street." She shuddered. "But then things really got crazy."

"What happened?"

"Suddenly, Miss McClain came out of her room, and she wasn't even decent!"

"Please, go on."

"Well, she was wearing this frilly little robe. Oh my…you could see right through it," she whispered.

"And?"

And she went back into Mr. Deane's bedroom!" she said, her eyes widening. "I almost fainted dead away. Can you imagine?"

Silent rage washed over his pallid face.

"I must be going." He quickly grabbed his hat and gloves and rushed out the door. The box of chocolates and flowers fell across the kitchen floor.

Jane Darby watched him leave from the parlor window. His carriage raced down the street. The sound of a cracking whip traveled on the wind. A satisfied smile lit up her face as Mr. Williams disappeared into the mist.

* * * *

Mara paused before releasing the final drop of color onto her canvas.

"Patrick, I'm finished with your portrait, if you'd like to take a look."

He crossed the room and stood by her side. His eyes traveled over the painting and his lips parted as he took a deep breath. He turned with a puzzled expression.

"Is it alright?"

"It's the most beautiful thing I've ever seen. Well, next to you that is." His eyes glistened as he reached down and took her hands. He studied them a moment and said, "I can't believe how talented you are, love. It truly is amazing. Sammy looks like a fine thoroughbred! But..." he hesitated, "that fellow in the picture can't be me?"

"Why do you say that?"

"Well, for starters, the bloke is too damn good looking!" But he grew serious, and his brow furrowed. "Do you really see me that way?"

"I do. Why, you're gorgeous." She smiled. Mara studied his face, trying to express something her words couldn't. "But it's the beauty of your soul that really speaks to me," she said, pointing towards his heart. His eyes filled with tears as he held her.

"You truly are a remarkable woman." He swept her up in his arms, kissing her softly, and then more urgently. He carried her over to a stack of hay bales, lowering her down onto the dried grass. Her hands gripped his broad shoulders, pulling him closer. He caressed her body, hesitating for a moment. She gazed back with a radiant smile, encouraging him to continue. Their eyes locked and his hand reached down, carefully loosening the buttons of her dress. Her blue eyes widened and pupils dilated. She exhaled with anticipation and whispered, "*Yes*". His mouth lifted at the corners, his eyes burned with passion. His fingers released the last fastener. She sighed deeply, and he pulled her closer, his mouth traveling over her neck and down to her breasts. His tongue flicked across supple curves, teeth grazing over the delicate skin. He pressed closer. Her hips arched against him, answering his desire. His hand reached under her dress, first exploring, and then satisfying the eager flesh. Mara leaned back, eyes half closed, biting down on her lower lip.

They were so enraptured with one another, that neither heard the footsteps. A shadow fell over them and Mara's eyes flew open. James Williams peered down, his face distorted by lunacy. She let out a scream. Patrick jumped, and looked over his shoulder. He hastily covered her up, blocking the intruder's view. She struggled for balance, clutching her bodice.

"What the hell are you doing here?" Patrick asked in outrage.

James' eyes were empty husks. He silently backed away into the shadows. His face was a mixture of rage and astonishment.

"Katie, so it's true, I see. You're a little whore after all."

Mara looked up in shock, and a flash of anger washed over her. "You have no right barging in on us. How dare you! I'm leasing this property. So, you're trespassing, and my name's not Katie. Get out!" She clutched her bodice, to keep it from falling back open. Tears welled up in her eyes, and her view became distorted. Patrick stood up, blocking her from James' leering gaze.

"Get the hell out of here, or I'll make sure you'll be needing a cane for the rest of your life," he hissed between clenched teeth. James slowly backed away. The corners of his mouth turned up, his eyes seething with hatred.

"Our little arrangement is over, my dear. I took a look at the repairs today, and they're not acceptable. So, your rent just got bumped up to one hundred dollars a month. If you can't pay the dues on time, I'm closing the gallery."

"You can't do that!" Her body shook, a cold tremor running down her spine.

"Oh, I most definitely can. There's a clause in the contract. If you don't believe me, you can ask Mr. Cohen at the bank. I have the right to raise your rent anytime I please. Maybe next time you might consider leaving business management to men, so you can stay on your back where you belong."

He turned to leave, and Patrick started to follow. Mara reached for his arm. "Please, don't go after him; he's just taunting, trying to get you in trouble." He turned back frustrated, and gathered her up in his arms. Her body shook, and she cried softly against him. He smoothed her hair back, and held her tightly. "Don't cry, little rose. This is my fault. I'm so sorry." He kissed the top of her head, holding her close.

"No, it's not," she said between short gasping breaths. "We're not doing anything wrong. You're my fiancé. Maybe we got a little carried away, but that doesn't give him the right to…" She couldn't finish the sentence and instead began to quietly sob against his chest.

He held her close until she stopped. She wiped at her face, and gingerly stood up. "Can we drive to the bank? I need to talk to Joshua to find out if the landlord can really raise my rent like he threatened."

Her mind raced as they drove down the street. Joshua Cohen smiled when they entered, but his face quickly turned to worry after seeing their expressions. He led them over to his desk and they took turns explaining James Williams' visit. They left out the part concerning their adventures in the hay. Joshua shook his head back and forth, and headed to the back, returning with a stack of paperwork. He thumbed through the documents.

"Damn it," he said, angrily. He looked up at Mara and quickly apologized for his language.

"Mr. Williams has been a loyal customer for some time. I never imagined that he would do anything so vicious. If I had known his intentions, I would have never arranged your meeting with him. I'm so very sorry."

"So, there's nothing that I can do about him raising the rent?"

Joshua's face grew solemn, his mouth pinched together. He tapped the desk with his pen, tracing his hands over the documents "Well, the problem is that he offered you a verbal agreement, to exchange labor for a reduction in the rent, but there's no rent control clause in your contract. The paperwork states that you'll be paying twenty-five dollars a month on the agreement that the appropriate repairs are to be completed in a timely fashion, but there's nothing legally preventing him from raising your rent. The agreement was on the honor system, and I'm afraid he's not proven to be an honorable man to say the least."

Mara looked down at her lap, biting the inside of her lip, "I see," she said softly.

Joshua looked back and forth at them. "Let me give you a few minutes to talk," he said quietly.

Patrick took her hand, "My fight's just around the corner. I can get the money."

She smiled up at him. "I don't want this to fall on you, love. I still have my gallery opening coming up. I started this business, and I really want to earn my way by paying my own bills."

"You're a stubborn little thing," he said, kissing her softly "We'll get through this. There are a lot of people standing behind you. We're going to figure this out."

They went back to the boarding house. At dinnertime, their housemates were quiet as Patrick explained what happened at the gallery.

"Why, it's outrageous," Jeremiah spoke up. "To take advantage of such a sweet young woman. It's unacceptable! He can't get away with it. I'm barring that monster from the store."

"Absolutely," Donald said, nodding his head vehemently.

Mara noticed that Jane Darby was absent from dinner that evening. It was a bit strange, but she was relieved that she wouldn't be there to gloat over her misfortune.

Betty reached over and put her hand on Mara's shoulder. We're going to work this out, honey. And just think, tomorrow people will be dropping by with their artworks at the gallery. You might find some wonderful pieces to sell."

Mara looked into her vivid green eyes. They were full of empathy and concern and she loved her for it. "I hope so. It's just that I'm worried about how far he'll go with this. What's stopping him from raising the rent again? He could keep doing it."

They were all quiet as they considered the possibility.

Sarah Levy put her hands together and leaned forward. "You can't worry about that now. Take it one step at a time. Try to focus on getting your paintings for the grand opening. Think about the rest later, and we're all here for you, Mara. You're a San Franciscan now. So, you're in good company."

They all nodded in earnest. She was grateful for their support, but her stomach felt like it was full of lead. She picked at her dinner, barely touching it. Her dreams that night were a mixture of losing the gallery and the shadow of her landlord's dark presence. His empty eyes were waiting.

Chapter 12

Mara awoke Friday morning with a sense of purpose. Patrick met her in the dining room for a quick breakfast before leaving the boarding house. The day was cold and bright as the carriage neared the gallery. Her heart raced as they turned the corner. A line had formed outside the door. Several men and women waited, most with paintings in their arms. She looked up at Patrick and he was grinning.

"Looks like the advertisement was a good idea, darlin'." Her hands shook as she climbed out of the cart. All eyes were on her as they walked over; she looked out at the crowd, trying to gather her thoughts.

"Thank you all for showing up today for our first painting call. My name is Mara McClain and I'm the owner of…" she hesitated a moment realizing that she had not named her gallery, "I'm the owner of *The Muse*." A murmur ran through the crowd, voices filled with curiosity and intrigue.

"We will be having our grand opening next Saturday. The pieces chosen today will be displayed and commissioned for this very special event. I'll be in the gallery office searching for works that best represent our great city. My associate, Mr. Deane, will call you in one at a time, so I can view your lovely artwork. Thank you very much for your cooperation. I'm looking forward to meeting each and every one of you."

A murmur ran through the crowd as she walked past. There was a sense of expectation in the air, a nervous excitement. It was a long day, and Mara examined many paintings. There were many levels of experience. Some of the artists were beginners, just discovering their craft, others were professionals, eager to show off their work and grateful for the chance. She was able to pick and choose from the best pieces. There was a variety of San Francisco scenes, portraiture, wildlife, and several landscape works. For the ones that weren't chosen, she gave words of encouragement, and advice on how to improve, suggesting they come back again in the future.

By noon, she had visitors from Mrs. Levy's house. Jeremiah and Donald brought their paintings, along with some extra chairs from the store. Betty and Joshua set up a card table, and went to work helping with commission contracts. Betty assisted by filling out the names of the artists and paintings, and then Jenjie arrived in the early afternoon. He had his canvases, along with a plate of sugar cakes from the restaurant. His mother had baked them special for Mara. He explained how proud his parents were to have him showing his work at the gallery. Sarah Levy arrived soon after with a basket of sandwiches and a pitcher of iced tea.

Soon, there were stacks of paintings in her office. Betty helped arrange them according to subject. Near sunset, her friends and clients slowly made their way back home. She looked around, took a deep breath, and stifled a yawn.

Patrick peeked inside and said, "You have one more artist that would like to speak with you."

She looked up as an elegantly dressed woman walked into the room. A forest green gown and matching hat complimented her dark hair and eyes. There was an air about her that made Mara take notice.

"Congratulations on opening your gallery, Mademoiselle McClain. It looks like you've had quite a success finding new pieces," she said, looking at the canvases organized throughout the room. She spoke with a heavy French accent. "Are you an artist as well as a business woman?"

"I am," she said. "I have a few of my works over here." Mara held up one of her oil paintings, a street scene from Philadelphia. It was a moody piece, displaying the setting sun, a row of buildings and people on their way home from work.

The visitor's eyes traveled over the canvas, taking in the delicate brushstrokes, the romantic air, and a day in the life scene, capturing the city's pulse.

"Yes, you most definitely are an artist."

"Thank you very much." She studied the woman with interest. Her dark hair and eyes were quite striking, her gaze direct.

"My name is Berthe Morisot. My home is in Paris, but I came to the states for a short holiday. I read about your gallery in the paper, and was quite excited to see that a woman happened to be the curator," she said. "I brought along a painting that I recently finished." She reached down by her chair and retrieved the canvas, placing it carefully on Mara's desk.

She studied the image. It was a rather small painting, a mother and child, sitting alone in a parlor. Short, rapid brushstrokes danced across the canvas. The contrast of white paint and dark hues accentuated the figures. The bold color choices regarding the mother's dress, and the child's dark hair allowed the figures to leap off the canvas, while the room itself was pushed far into the background. The outer edges of the painting were unfinished, giving the composition a free and spontaneous appearance.

"Oh, my, this is truly remarkable. You know, there's something about your brushstrokes that seem so familiar. My friend recently showed me a photograph of the work of an artist from Paris. His name is Claude Monet. Your painting is quite different, both in subject and substance and yet, there is a similar sense of freedom, a feeling of abandonment. Your art depicts a powerful intimacy between the mother and child. It's as if you're allowing the viewer into a secret world. You've actually captured the essence of love. It's incredible…beautiful."

"Thank you. That's very kind. A smile flickered. "Oh, and Claude Monet, yes, we're old friends. He's quite the artist, a bit on the obsessive side…though, aren't we all?"

Mara nodded in agreement, an unspoken understanding between them.

"He's been known to paint the same church from morning to sundown just to capture the changing light. I'm afraid I do most of my painting inside the home. Paris is transforming itself right before our eyes. It's quite hectic at times. It seems that there's a new building or street every time I leave the house." She was quiet for a moment, looking out the window.

"I admire you, Mademoiselle McClain. It's not easy to stake a claim in this world; men run it, and we have to tread ever so lightly, but you're doing it, aren't you? Never let anyone say you can't. Always remember that, chéri." They looked at each other, speaking without words.

Mara sensed she was in the presence of someone special, although she wouldn't fully understand it until many years later, after she'd read about the *French Impressionist Movement* and discovered how her new friend, Berthe Morisot, was one of the founding artists, and a leader in her circle. They'd exchanged addresses that afternoon and would continue to write to one other for the rest of their lives, their friendship growing stronger with each passing year, a window into the ever-changing French art society.

The words she spoke that day helped to strengthen her resolve to go forward with her gallery. When her key locked the door, Mara had a new sense of determination. She had no trouble sleeping that night.

BOOK TWO

The Barbary Coast

Samuel Johnson was a giant of a man. Born and raised in San Francisco at the height of the Gold Rush, his father an escaped felon, his mother was a prostitute from one of the city's original whorehouses. He'd been raised on the streets, and had been sheltered from nothing. He knew all the johns by name, and the house Madame, Aunt Dottie, was like a second mother. Sometimes, she gave him candy and sent him out to play if his own mom was entertaining a gentleman caller. He knew nothing different, and his childhood was a fairly happy one, but children are cruel, and at the age of nine, neighborhood boys started calling him a bastard and his mother a whore. He asked around until he learned what the words meant, and he went back to the boys later that day and proceeded to beat them bloody, leaving them covered in tears with a few broken bones. When their blood flowed red, it stirred something in him. It was a nice feeling, peaceful in a way. You see, he never really felt alive until that moment. Once he saw those first scarlet drops, he was thirsty. He searched for it, and was often successful. Over the next seven years, he would be in and out of jail cells, accused of fighting, stealing, anything that would give him a little release. This was his life, and it was all right.

On his sixteenth birthday, he sat alone in a cold cell, one he'd become quite familiar with over the years. He was studying his bloody hands and didn't hear the footsteps. When he looked up, he realized he had a visitor. He eyed him suspiciously, wondering if he might be one of those fancy boys that seemed to seek him out for his favors. It wasn't the first time he'd been approached, and when money was tight…well…if it was good enough for his old mother, he supposed it was good enough for him, too.

But this wasn't the gentleman's pleasure. He was a shorter man, with a shock of blond hair, a streak of white running across it. He had a heavy British accent and a strange air, but there was something about him Samuel liked; maybe it was the way his eyes were dark and empty, not unlike his own. The man bailed him out that night; money was no object.

He took him down to Chinatown, bought him some food, and made a proposition. He wanted to sponsor him, he explained. He didn't understand that word, and so the stranger slowly and carefully described his intentions. He liked to watch fights, he enjoyed betting on them and he had the money to do it, and had been doing it since he'd moved to the states, but he wanted to get a little closer to the action, and decided he was going to take a boxer under his wing. He would provide him a place to stay; his meals would be taken care of, and maybe a few extras. When he asked what those were, he just smiled and told him he would show him tonight.

In exchange for paying his way, he would fight for him. His eyes lit up. Yes, he was going to learn to fight professionally. He wasn't sure what this entailed, but it was all right. He would get his bills paid just for fighting. What could be better? However, there were some rules. He must never speak his manager's name or show any signs of knowing him. That night, his new sponsor took him down to a dark building in Chinatown. When the red doors opened, his eyes widened. Striking women welcomed them inside. They wore skin-hugging dresses, and smiled with dark red lips, their eyes the color of raven wings. Shiny black locks curtained down their delicate shoulders. The room was hazy with smoke, curling up around him like a lover's embrace.

He was led into a back room and presented with a pipe. A young girl handed it to him, her eyes the color of onyx. He took a drag and discovered paradise. The last thing he remembered was his new manager leaving the room. He put arms around two of the most beautiful women he'd ever seen. They appeared to be twins. As the opium surged through his veins, he saw heaven, and knew that he would do anything for the feeling to stay. For the remainder of his short life, he would seek that high, and nothing would prevent him from getting it, no deed too dark, no action too shameful. For the next five years, he boxed in matches in the dark hovels and basements of Kearny Street. He made a name for himself. Other boxers kept their distance. He was known for fighting dirty, and enjoyed it when he seriously injured his opponents, once even killing a man. He had no friends other than his associates at the opium den, and that was all right by him. His love was for the pipe. It was what got him up in the morning, and it was what he dreamed of at night.

On this particular evening, he sat on the ground, outside the ring, drenched in sweat, bloody, but victorious. He knew his biggest fight was just around the corner. It was going to be a payday like no other. He was glad; he needed money to get high. It took a lot more these days to make a dent. His savings were gone, and he was in desperate need. The itchiness was beginning to spread over his skin. He'd scratched himself raw, making deep red gashes on his legs, where his fingernails had ripped off patches of skin. He looked down at the floor taking in shallow breaths. A shadow fell over his body, and he looked up. James Williams stood over him, a tight smile on his face.

"You're looking a little piqued, my friend. Looks like you could use a pick me up. Congratulations on your win by the way. You've almost made it to the top. There's just one more fight to become champion. You'll earn quite a bit of money when this happens, but it looks like you might need some now."

"Could you lend me a little, sir?" he asked, a whine in his voice that he couldn't quite hide.

"That might be arranged, but I'll need something in exchange."

His eyes lifted, questioning.

"Next Saturday, you're going to meet a new opponent. His name is Patrick Deane. He's an Irish bastard. Yes, a real piece of work. So, I want you to do something for me."

His eyes were slowly closing, as the pain in his gut deepened, he needed a fix and he needed it bad.

"Pay attention," James said calmly, slapping him hard across the face. He sat bolt upright, his eyes blazing with anger.

"Wipe that scowl off before I change my mind about giving you an advance."

He looked sheepishly at the floor like a scolded puppy.

"That's better."

"Now, this is what you need to do for me. You're going to hurt this Patrick Deane. You're going to hurt him bad."

His eyes lit up. He nodded eagerly

"And, one thing more. You know there's some new product at your favorite Oriental market. I believe it's called *Maiden Flower?*"

"He eyed him greedily.

"Let's just say if you actually killed this Patrick Deane, well then…perhaps, I might just gift you with a generous payment of this new flavor."

His eyes glimmered.

"I can do that, boss, I'd like to do it for you, sir," he said, cloyingly.

"Very good, boy. Why don't we get you a little relief then?" His smiled widened, as James put his arm around his shoulders, leading him outside.

The Grand Opening

Mara paced back and forth trying to calm herself. It was six o'clock and people would be arriving within the hour. The canvases were hung along the walls, each according to subject and artist. Jenjie's paintings were arranged across the green partition, each animal representing its zodiac year. Underneath the images were small cards describing their significance. Donald's Triptych was set near the front window, showing the San Francisco Bay in all its glory. Berthe Morisot's piece was on the opposite end, a private glimpse into the French art scene. Mara scattered a few of her own canvases around the room. She'd placed them among her new clients' works. Her friends took turns tidying up and preparing the appetizers. Mrs. Levy brought along finger foods—deviled eggs and vegetable latkes. Donald and Jeremiah had donated a few bottles of champagne for the guests. Jenjie was hanging a small landscape scene of the Oakland Train Station. Betty and Joshua were busy pinning streamers along the walls. Teenage boys lit street lamps down the avenue. A heavy fog was rolling in, making everything appear hazy and distant. Mara looked out at the darkening street, anticipating the visitors. Patrick walked up behind her, put his hands on her shoulders, and kissed her neck. She smiled and reached back, folding her hands over his.

"I'm so proud of you, Mara. You're quite the business woman."

She turned to him, her eyes moist with tears. "Thank you. I couldn't have done this without you, and just look at how our friends helped to put this together. I can't begin to tell you how grateful I am."

"I wish I could stay for the whole thing."

"It's alright. I know you have to prepare for the fight. We're all going to come down to watch it later tonight," she said, her mouth trembling slightly.

"That means the world to me, love, but I don't want you to be frightened when you see the match. It can look worse than it is," he trailed off.

She did her best to reassure him, but her insides felt cold. Mara forced a smile, trying to put him at ease.

* * * *

The guests arrived in twos and threes, larger groups within the hour. Joshua made his way over to the open door with a violin in hand. He handled the instrument with great love, and the music flowed forth with an intimate grace. It was a stirring melody, soft and sweet. Betty moved closer, losing herself in his aquamarine eyes. A smile moved over his face. Neither spoke, as no words were needed.

Several visitors huddled around Donald's paintings. Whenever someone new approached, he would hold his breath. A well-dressed gentleman made his way over to the window. He studied the triptych with his hand resting against his beard. He turned and introduced himself as Mayor Thomas H. Shelby. Mara and Donald exchanged shocked expressions. He went on to explain how he was impressed with the new gallery, and that he was very taken with Donald's work. He asked if he might purchase the entire set, describing how the paintings would be perfect for his downtown office. Mr. Becker's eyes widened as he struggled for words. The mayor patiently waited for his answer. He took a deep breath and said it would be an honor. Mayor Shelby shook his hand, and gave Donald a firm pat on the shoulder. Jeremiah stood behind him with a proud smile.

Mara busied herself mingling with her guests and was embraced eagerly by her peers. Donald and Jenjie were treated like royalty that evening, everyone wanted to meet them, some even asking for autographs. There was quite an interest in Mara's paintings as well. She'd sold the majority of the collection by the end of the evening. Berthe Morisot didn't make it to the opening that night, instead she was on her way back to Paris for an exhibition. Mara looked forward to writing her that the grand opening had been a success. At the end of the evening, an elderly gentleman made his way around the room, taking his time, studying each piece with interest. He was so taken with Berthe Morisot's painting that he not only wanted to purchase it, but also insisted on donating fifty dollars towards the gallery as a sponsor of the arts. Mara made enough money from the paintings to pay three months' rent. It was a relief, and she couldn't have been happier.

By ten o'clock the final guests had departed. Her friends took turns congratulating her. Sarah Levy went to the back of the room, retrieved the last champagne bottle, and filled their glasses.

"To Mara McClain," she said, raising a toast, "Congratulations on your first art opening. We couldn't be more proud of you. Cheers to many more!"

"Mazel tov," her friends cried in unison.

"Mara looked out at the kind faces, her body shaking with emotion. "I wish I could find the words to thank you for everything you've done for me these past few weeks. Each and every one of you is a part of my family now, and I love you all." Her voice shook, cracking on the last few words.

After taking turns toasting, the friends made their way to Kearny Street to support Patrick's final fight. Joshua helped Mara and Betty inside his carriage. A few moments into the ride, Mara looked over at her friends and realized they were holding hands. She smiled as they made their way into the dark, cold night.

Patrick Deane

Patrick stood alone in the back room. He heard the laughter and excitement of the crowds outside. They were slowly taking their seats, anxious for the festivities to begin. It was by far the largest gathering of any fight he'd ever been in. Most of his matches took place in back alleys, or hidden deep within San Francisco's underground, but this time, things were different. Some of the wealthiest people in the city—politicians, bankers and businessmen were involved. With a little money exchanged here and there, the fight would take place right out in the open. High society wanted to play, and the event grew into quite the formal affair. *The Golden Queen Casino* stepped up to host the match. They'd moved their gambling tables downstairs, clearing out the entire second floor. Velvet backed chairs were arranged around a large roped in arena. An open bar available for those who'd invested high stakes in the game. Gentleman and well-dressed ladies walked about the room, engaging in polite conversation. Their soft laughter was more suited to the theatre than the violent affair about to take place.

The room's periphery held an entirely different crowd. These were the hardened gamblers, the brothel owners, and drug dealers. Five of their highest-ranking leaders represented the Chinese Tongs. They stood together, dressed in identical black attire. They surveyed the room as a united front. Their emotionless faces gave no clue to their power and influence. The Tongs simultaneously aided their people and enslaved them. They offered protection against rising discrimination, but in doing so, demanded a heavy price. When these restitutions were not met, punishments are carried out swiftly and violently. They had their hands in many pies—opium dens, prostitution rings, gambling parlors, along with their racketeering. On these accounts, they were given a wide berth.

Across from this somber group stood a middle-aged woman with an aura of eternal youth. Lola Vilonia was the Madame and proprietor of *Lola's Ladies*. Her pink hotel was one of the town's most infamous brothels. The men hovered around her like a queen bee, and she busied herself keeping court. She wore a pink taffeta gown, low cut, leaving little to the imagination. Every so often, one of the more well to do businessmen would gaze in her direction, making it apparent that it was not the first time he'd looked into those ebony eyes. Her mouth would turn up, and she'd smile her secret smile.

Ordinarily these outsiders were looked down upon, if not openly despised by the upper class, but tonight everyone was welcome inside the *Golden Queen*. These people were in charge of all of the forbidden pleasures of the city. In the light of day, the wealthy aristocrats made every point to ignore their very existence, but at night, things were different. They begrudgingly put up with their presence in order to indulge in a little thrill, an exciting jaunt inside the darker corners of San Francisco's Barbary Coast. In any other situation, their paths would never cross; this was how each side liked it, but on this night, on account of necessity, their worlds collided. The entire top floor of the casino was decked out and ready to house as many guests as they could squeeze in. They had moved several gambling tables to accommodate the fight and the room was packed.

The bets were placed, and the winner was going to take home a pay day like no other. The purse was large enough for Patrick to change his life, and he would take it, gladly. There would be a small part of him that would miss the excitement of the ring—the thrill of victory, but he knew he couldn't keep this up. He would need to protect his hands for his new businesses, but more importantly, he had to do it for Mara. She was his life now; his very soul lived for her smile, the way her eyes lit up when he touched her, the passion they shared. She was just a tiny little thing, but her heart and mind were so strong, and she stirred something in him, something he'd never known existed. He would fight for her tonight, and then his boxing career would come to an end. He just couldn't stand the pain in her eyes, or the way her tears surfaced when she studied his bruises. He tried to reassure her, and insisted it was nothing, but it just was too much for her. So, this would be his last fight. It was as simple as that. He'd give her a good life.

He understood that she wanted to be an independent businesswoman, but as a man, he meant to provide for her, and provide he would. He noticed the way her eyes lit up when she looked at the Painted Lady. Oh, God, the way she talked about the autumn colors, and it being like a fairytale, and her eyes became so wistful. Those beautiful blue eyes. His heart ached every time he looked at them. He wondered if she really understood the depth of his love for her. He'd give his life if she asked, his very soul. He would get her that house. He'd build it with his own two hands. Oh, yes, he would, and together they would start their lives together, raise a beautiful family, and eventually they would grow old, happy in their love and memories. He imagined their children and grandchildren, even their great grandchildren running through the house, playing up and down the stairs. Their laughter would ring like little bells, happy and safe inside the towering walls. There would be lots of rooms for them to play. He hoped that *Autumn Lady* would be their legacy, passed down from generation to generation. He would see to every detail of the estate, and it would be remarkable. Stained glass windows surrounded the parlor, fall leaves etched in the glass, turning the light into the color of Mara's strawberry-blond curls.

And of course, he would build a beautiful art studio for his bride. There would be lots of windows for her to paint by, and there would be roses outside. Yes, he would plant rose bushes all over the yard, roses for his lovely Irish rose. This is what he would do for her. She was his life now and he would provide everything her heart desired. And he'd protect her too. Maybe, he could even manage to purchase the building for her gallery, or perhaps he would just build her one. He wouldn't let James anywhere near Mara. He'd already taken steps to protect her from that monster. He'd informed Sheriff Carpenter all about Mr. Williams' dark past, and his friend had done some excellent detective work. He'd recently discovered that James had his hands in a lot of illegal business dealings, had in fact been involved in gambling to the point of losing quite a bit of money. He was deep in debt in the Chinese community. The sheriff had explained how he enjoyed the opium houses, the women, and the drugs. So much so, that he was losing more than he was making off of his real-estate investments. Patrick wondered if James had placed money on this fight. It would be ironic if he had. Because he was going to win and he hoped that meant that the man would lose all of his savings. If all went well, the sheriff just might be able to arrest Mr. Williams tonight, if not for the murders, then for the illegal dealings he was involved in around San Francisco.

So, he began to warm up, taking quick jabs into the air. Outside, the noise of the swelling crowd grew to a roar. He imagined that Mara and their friends were in their seats by now—anxiously waiting. He hoped to finish the fight quickly and be done with it, then they could start their new lives together. Patrick couldn't wait to hold her in his arms again.

James Williams

James Williams sat near the front of the ring, a thin smile on his face. Jane Darby was curled up against him, her considerable bosom pressing close. She batted her eyelashes, pursed her lips, trying desperately to be engaging. She was a good-looking woman. Her chest went on for miles, and he planned to get his fill. He realized she wasn't actually interested in him, just his money. That was all right. Because he only wanted one thing from the ditzy Southern belle, and that was her body. He intended to take it all, and when he was done, she would be tossed aside like the whores from Chinatown. It would be easy, he imagined, but just in case she wanted to pretend to be a lady, he had plans to help ease her inhibitions. He had brought along a helper. He would convince her to take a little sample from his opium pipe. A taste of the *Maiden Flower* would ease her nerves. James had little doubt she would cooperate. She was set on pleasing him. Oh, and she would please him. It would be like taking candy from a baby. A smile spread over his face as he looked down at her breasts. Yes, just like candy from a baby.

His smile slowly faded as his mind wandered back to Mara McClain. He planned to raise her rent again, soon. He looked forward to seeing the light go out of her eyes when he gave her the news. This time, she wouldn't have her Irish bastard there to protect her. He'd be six feet under by then. He wasn't going to leave this fight alive if he had anything to do with it. James had invested most of his savings betting on Samuel. The boy would do his job, earning him a small fortune in the process, and he'd be able to pay off all of his debts. Killing Patrick would change his life in so many wonderful ways. The thought made him happy, and a thin smile slowly emerged. His thoughts trickled back to Mara. He wondered just how desperate she would be to save her gallery. Yes, perhaps then they could work out some kind of arrangement. The thought stirred him, and he let out a contented sigh. Jane Darby snuggled close, whispering cloying words in his ear. Yes, it was going to be a good night tonight, a good night indeed.

* * * *

Mara sat down next to Betty, close to the ring. Joshua, Jeremiah, Donald, and Sarah followed. She looked at the empty mat realizing that at any moment Patrick would walk out with his opponent. She closed her eyes, praying he'd be safe and that the fight would end quickly. When she looked back up, she noticed the people sitting on the opposite side. A cold shiver went down her spine. James Williams was staring, a thin smile on his face. She quickly looked away, her heart pounding. *What was he doing here? And Jane Darby was sitting by his side, arms wrapped around him, whispering in his ear.*

As much as she disliked the girl, she was struck with an overwhelming sense of pity for her. *Did she have any idea what kind of man he was?* She took a deep breath, making up her mind to talk to Miss Darby after the fight. She had the right to know that she was keeping company with a monster. She turned to her right and looked at her best friend. Betty was gazing up at Joshua. They seemed completely oblivious that the fight was about to take place. He kissed her hand, and then placed his arm carefully around her shoulder. Mara looked away, happy that they'd found one another. She took a deep breath and tried to put the fight in God's hands. If they could get through this night, they could get through anything. She just wished she could shake her uneasy feeling. A murmuring ran through the crowd, the wave of excitement intensified. The fighters were on their way out.

Samuel Johnson

Samuel sat in the corner waiting. He'd had a busy week sparring in the days and smoking *Maiden Flower* in the evenings. It was beginning to take its toll—blood in the sink every morning, and the lethargy was worsening. Luckily his sponsor had shown him a special way that helps him with that. He couldn't fight very well after spending too many nights in paradise. So, his boss showed him a trick. Now Samuel was never very fond of needles, but he reassured him that it would make him feel better, and boy did it. He taught him to tape up his arm, tap his vein a little, and stick the needle in. He always had to make sure to push on the handle because there were bad bubbles that might want to kill him. He remembered his first time like it was yesterday. There was a little pinch, but he soon forgot all about it. Because this new drug, this cocaine they called it, was like liquid fire. It burned in his veins, and then he felt like God—and maybe he was. He took his first opponent down within minutes. He really enjoyed the way his head had snapped back, and how hard he'd fallen. It was quite nice, this new drug. His sponsor had promised him plenty more where that came from. Lately, he'd been thinking it might be kind of fun to shoot a little cocaine with a bit of the *Maiden Flower*. *Wouldn't that be interesting?* The thought gave him a tightening sensation down below. He looked forward to visiting *The Red Doors* after the fight. With all his new money, he could afford a girl or two— maybe three. They had a couple of fresh ones recently arrived from Beijing. Might have to have a real party tonight. Yes, he would. He deserved it.

Samuel had passed his new opponent earlier in the evening. He had no doubt that he could take him down easily. He wasn't sure about killing him the first round though. This fighter had one of those pretty boy faces that reminded him of one of his old clients. He'd like to rearrange that pretty face. Yes, he'd like that very much. He'd start with his little pug nose. Yeah. He imagined it flattening under his fist. Smash. Blood would go everywhere. It would be fun to see the look of pain and surprise. The tightening sensation started again. Yes, he would definitely be buying some girls tonight.

After his nose was broken, he'd slowly break him down, little by little, nice and slow. It's what the boss wanted. Might even earn him a little extra for taking his time. He loved his sponsor. Yes. Sometimes he hated him, but mostly he loved him. He was the father he'd always dreamed of. He took care of everything, even when he screwed up. Like that time he killed that boxer in the alley. He was a black fellow, big as a house. He wouldn't go down no matter how hard he tried. An hour in and he was still swinging. Samuel was exhausted, and the man was showing no signs of slowing. Well, he was starting to get real itchy by that time, really craving a fix. He wanted to speed things along. So he circled him for several minutes, playing with him, putting him off balance, and then he went for it; punched him right in the throat. His opponent froze where he stood, his hands clutching his neck. There was a lot of blood. Oh, yes. It flowed like a river, down his chest, pooling around his feet. The boxer went to his knees, gurgling, clawing at his throat. The blood was eventually replaced by a gush of white foam. Samuel enjoyed the blood more, but the foam was pretty interesting. Well, the man never got his air back. He was dead by the time Samuel had stepped out of the alley.

His boss wasn't happy about it either. He spent quite a bit of money to make the man disappear, but he fixed it, and he was able to keep on fighting. Samuel noticed the other boxers stayed away from him after that, avoided looking him in the eyes, but that was all right. Because he still had his sponsor, and yes, he did love the man. His boss would explain things in a way he could understand, without those big words that always made his head hurt. He was good like that. Kind of patient, he was. Although he wasn't allowed to call him by his real name, sometimes when his boss was in a good mood, after winning a big purse, he'd let him call him *Pops*. At night Samuel would dream that he called him *dad* right out in the open where everyone could hear. He'd take his hand, and they'd enjoy a little bit of heaven. Yeah. Life was pretty good. He sat and waited. Almost time. He'd make his *Pops* proud. Maybe tonight, he'd let him call him *dad,* and then they'd go celebrate together inside *The Red Doors*.

The Fight

The crowd rose to their feet when Patrick and Samuel walked into the room. They entered from separate corners. Patrick wore an emerald robe over his trousers. Donald had made a present of it earlier that evening. He wanted his friend to be represented in style and had been working on it for some time. Painting happened to be only one of Mr. Becker's talents, the needle being the other. Everyone was quite impressed with the fabric's quality and design. Mara admired the large white shamrock on the back and his last name embroidered in bold letters. Ireland would definitely be represented tonight. Donald smiled modestly at their praise. He hoped that the robe would give his friend a little luck.

Samuel wore black. There was no design or writing on his robe. It looked more like a funeral cape. Both men were shirtless. The coaches followed their charges as they climbed under the golden ropes. Jenjie was behind Patrick; an elderly man followed Samuel. The men disrobed and were given a few words of instruction.

The fighters warmed up in their corners, pacing, jabbing at air.

An attractive woman with a curtain of blond curls made her way toward the front of the room. She climbed beneath the golden ropes, and the crowd went wild, showing their appreciation with ear piercing whistles and catcalls.

Goldie Donahue was the *Golden Queen* in both spirit and essence. She was in her early forties, but her baby doll face was fresh and youthful. Hazel eyes glimmered in the lights. She looked out at her audience, seeming to know each and every one of her patrons. She was a tall woman, with long legs and an hourglass figure. Her golden gown flickered with a thousand teardrop sequins. Blond curls bounced around her head as she waved to her adoring fans. She'd put her heart and soul into the casino. It was the only child she'd ever have, and that was fine by her. She'd pulled many strings, and extended quite a few favors to make this fight happen, but now that it had, she was ready to sit back and enjoy. She would make a pretty penny tonight. Goldie looked out at the crowd, her white teeth flashing like shiny pearls. It looked as if the entire city had come out to play. She was ready to give them the fight of their life. It took several minutes for the audience to settle down. She stood in the middle of the mat and stretched her golden-gloved arms outward, eagerly welcoming them all. A wave of cheering followed, along with whistling and applause. When it finally quieted down, she continued.

"I'd like to thank you all for coming out to join us for our very first boxing championship at *The Golden Queen Casino*. We're so very proud to host this special event for you fine ladies and gentleman. We hope many of you will stay afterwards and enjoy the festivities down below."

Loud whistling and cheering echoed around the room.

One man stood on his chair and hollered, "I want you to help me with my festivities down below, Goldie darling!"

This brought another roar of laughter and applause. Several men pounded on their tables. She walked toward the front of the ring, her hips swishing from side to side.

"Johnny, you just show me your big golden nuggets, and then maybe we can talk about it." She winked.

The crowd lost it, hollering and cheering. The man blew her a kiss and sat back down.

After the noise died, she went on, a radiant smile lighting up her face.

"Now, I know that you're all eager to get this show going. So, let's get this party started! Tonight, ladies and gentleman, two of our very own San Franciscan boys will be facing each other in the fight of their lives.

"This competition may be a little different then what some of you are used to. You won't be seeing the same rules and regulations associated with standard boxing. In the spirit of true bare-knuckle fighting, we want to stay close to tradition. So, tonight, there's no rules, rounds or referees. It's anything goes! There will be one exception to this free-for-all. I will be counting down to ten for any boxer that falls to the mat and does not make it back to his feet. The winner will be the last man standing. My friends get ready for the fight of the century!"

Applause exploded.

"In the left corner, wearing emerald green, a true Irish gentleman, and ladies, a handsome one for sure! Please put your hands together for Patrick Deane!" People clapped and cheered. Some stamped their feet. "Mr. Deane is fighting today as an undefeated champion, at six foot two, weighing in at one hundred seventy-eight pounds.

"In the far right corner is Samuel Johnson, a Kearny Street native, six feet, six inches, and weighing in at a whopping one hundred and ninety-eight pounds. He's a true San Franciscan giant. Please give him a warm welcome!"

A few clapped, others murmured, and several booed. His legacy was dark, and his fans were few.

"When I ring this little golden bell, it's time to come out fighting. Good luck, gentleman."

She climbed over the ropes and stood outside the ring.

* * * *

The two opponents jumped around their corners warming up. Samuel caught Patrick's eyes, giving him a dark smile. There were several black holes where his teeth should have been, his gums decayed and bloody.

The bell rang, and the two men raced toward one another. Patrick was light on his feet, moving swiftly along the mat, studying his opponent with experienced eyes. He was aware of his past, and knew he was bound to play dirty. Samuel was a lumbering giant, with an arm span several inches longer than his, but he was all bulk, not an athlete. And there was another thing. Jenjie had learned that the fighter was compromised, a hard-core drug addict. It was written all over his face. So, even if he outweighed him by more than twenty pounds, and was several inches taller, he was certain that he could beat him with endurance and intellect.

So, he danced around him, arms held high, teasing him into swinging, and then backing off every time he came close. This worked pretty well for the first few minutes or so, each fighter getting in some punches, but nothing too serious. Patrick could already see the shadow of fatigue on Samuel's sweaty face, the dark shadows under his eyes, but there was one thing Patrick didn't consider while they paced one another taking jabs. It was the blind rage that the man had for him, or the cocaine flowing through his veins, just beginning to gather and pulse. Like a bomb, the man was getting ready to explode, and he was thirsty for his blood. Yes, Samuel was not seeing enough scarlet tonight and it was frustrating him. He wanted the pretty boy to bleed, and he needed to win, so he and *Pops* could go visit *The Red Doors,* and this boxer was too damn fast.

Then it happened. Samuel eyes lit up as a burst of energy flowed through his body. His arm swung back, and he hurled it forward, striking Patrick square in the nose. Blazing pain exploded behind Patrick's eyes. A spray of blood spattered across the room, some of it landing on Jane Darby's pretty pink dress. She screamed as the droplets hit the fabric. For Patrick, it was like being hit by a bag of bricks, he heard the sound of cartilage snapping, only vaguely aware that it was coming from his own face, and then there was the pain. It was sharp, alive. A wave of nausea gripped him. The blood was warm and sticky, and he tasted its coppery flavor on his tongue. He was vaguely aware of his name being screamed out over and over again. It was Mara's voice. His love was crying for him. He wiped at the blood, as another wave of pain almost took him to the ground. It was pouring out like a faucet. From the corner of his eye he could see James Williams, grinning, clapping. Jane Darby's arms were wrapped around him, a satisfied smile on her face.

Then his opponent began to laugh, it was a strange sound, something he'd never imagined hearing during a fight. For a man his size, it should have been deep and low, but instead it came out like a high-pitched giggle.

"Did you like that, pretty boy? Did you? Not so pretty anymore are you? I'm going to make you bleed, you Irish bastard. My pops wants you to hurt."

Patrick tried his best to ignore the taunting. He had no idea what he was talking about, and he didn't want to. He continued on with a succession of right jabs, but it was getting more and more difficult to breathe; the blood was going down his throat in thick clots, which he tried spitting out on the mat. A feeling of panic washed over him when he couldn't get his breath.

Jenjie called out to him from the corner, "Get back to your center,

Patrick. Try to stay calm. You've got this. Don't worry. You'll get your breath back. Focus."

He spit out a mouthful of blood, trying to ease his body through the pain. Yes, Jenjie was right. He had to stay calm. He tried to steady his breathing. *Get back into the zone.* He struck out again with everything he had, jabbing in rapid fire. He raised his fists high, pummeling Samuel with a series of uppercuts. His head snapped back and forth, but his opponent just stared back in dull surprise. Patrick was dumbfounded. The man should have been down on the floor unconscious, but instead he just lumbered around the ring with an idiotic grin on his face. So, they kept at it, back and forth like two dancers. Patrick was slowly getting his breath back. He landed several more blows to Samuel's face, chest and stomach. He'd hear an occasional groan, but nothing really seemed to faze him. He'd strike him hard, and Samuel continued to just smile without any signs of slowing down. They traded blows back and forth, and to Patrick's bewilderment, it looked like Samuel was becoming more energized. He was beginning to get the upper hand, laying in some hard hits to his face and chest. Blood was running freely now, into his eyes and out of his mouth, and then there was a brilliant flash of light as Samuel pummeled him across the jaw. He lost his footing, slipping in a pool of blood and fell. With his hands on the ropes, he struggled for balance.

Samuel came up behind him. He grabbed him around the throat, and his other hand laid in a series of punches to his kidneys. There was an agonizing bolt of pain. He cried out weakly, and was answered by a high-pitched squeal of laughter. Booing rumbled through the crowd, people had come for a fight, but many weren't prepared for this level of violence. Patrick slipped in his own blood as a cramping gripped his insides. A thousand knives pierced him. Samuel's shadow descended, and he continued to punch and kick him while he was down on the mat. The crowd roared with excitement. He pummeled him with a series of blows to the back of his head. Women were screaming and men calling to stop the fight, but none came forward. So, Samuel continued on with the abuse. He reached down, and picked him off the ground by his hair, then struck him hard across the jaw. When he released Patrick, he fell to the ground motionless, but this was not enough for Samuel. He followed it with a swift kick to the face. The tip of his shoe caught him under the right eye. A bolt a light flashed in his head, and his eye swelled shut. Patrick crawled around the mat, unable to see.

The pain was unbearable and the blanket of gray washed over him. There was a pounding in his ears and the room was slowly closing in. He felt like he was floating. The overwhelming desire was to just lie down and go to sleep, anything to escape the pain, but there was a voice in the distance, and it belonged to his beloved. Hearing it made him want to fight just a little bit more.

Meanwhile, Goldie Donahue had made her way back over to the arena. She held out her arms toward the boxers. Her voice was loud and clear, counting up to ten, "One, two, three…"

Patrick crawled blindly around the mat, reaching for the ropes. Each time he tried to stand a bolt of pain ran down his spine. He opened his mouth, and a bubble of blood escaped his lips. A thin beam of light guided him. He moved toward it, straining in the dark. His left eye was hazy, but he could make out the shadow of James Williams' face. It was a mask of pure ecstasy. Williams suddenly leapt to his feet and shouted, "Kill him, son, kill him for me!"

Samuel calmly walked over, looked down. "My dad says it's time for you to die."

Patrick Deane

Patrick would never fully understand how he'd managed to get back on his feet, or how he found the strength to exert himself, but when he was a very old man, resting alongside his beloved, he would remember this day and realize it was her voice that had determined their destiny. When he heard it, he knew he must help her.

Mara was standing on her chair, screaming his name, begging for someone to stop the fight. Her friends had their arms around her, and their tears were flowing. She eventually managed to break free, pushing her way over to the ring. Jenjie caught her before she crawled underneath the ropes. He held her, his hands wrapped around her waist. He did his best to soothe his friend, whispering in her ear and rubbing her shoulders. He'd been trying to stop the fight, but no one would listen. There was too much money to be made. So, he just held onto her while she leaned towards the ropes, grasping. It was all he could do.

"Patrick!" She screamed over and over, reaching for him in vain. With his one good eye, he saw her. Mara was sobbing, she needed him, and so he stumbled until he was back on his feet. He began to strike out, clumsy at first, but he was determined. He missed the first few times, but he eventually found his rhythm. Samuel smiled and taunted, but with a flicker of uncertainty.

* * * *

Once he realized that Patrick wasn't giving up, he became afraid. Fists were coming at him from every direction, and the blows he took were painful…so excruciatingly painful. The cocaine in his system was fading, he no longer felt like God. In fact, he felt tired. His body hurt, oh, it hurt so much. Each punch peeled away another layer of his determination, another layer of courage. Patrick continued to pound away.

Samuel took the abuse as long as he could, his giant body wracked in agony, and then he could take no more. He tried to retreat to the far side of the ring, but Patrick followed. Now, it was his turn to bleed. A shower of punches rained down, opening fresh cuts and bruises. He saw his own blood flowing towards the ground. It poured freely from his mouth and nose. He stumbled around, looking for a way out. Patrick grabbed him by the shoulder, turning him back around. He reached his fist behind his head, and let out a hard uppercut to his jaw. A spray of blood flew onto the crowd, generating more screaming and cheering. People were on their feet now, chanting Patrick's name, the sound growing in volume, pulsing out like a giant heartbeat. Samuel's body crumbled beneath him, the last of his willpower destroyed. He curled up in a fetal position, his hands over his head. Two bodyguards, each holding one of her arms, led Goldie through the frenzied crowd. They lifted her up onto a velvet chair, supporting her around her waist, a satisfied smile on her face. She raised her gloved arms high into the air and began counting up, "One, two, three…" Each number encouraged more cheering and foot stomping. When she announced "ten", the audience roared, hats and coins were tossed into the air. Others simply stared into space, realizing the fortunes they'd lost.

"Congratulations, Mr. Deane! You are the light-heavy weight champion of the Golden Queen Casino! First round of drinks on the house!" This caused another eruption of cheering and table pounding.

As Samuel's eyes were closing, he looked out into the crowd of faces, searching for *Pops*, but he was long gone. Samuel didn't realize that tonight was the very last time he'd ever see him, and perhaps that was for the best. Because later that evening, he would take his last bit of cocaine and mix it with a little *Maiden Flower*. At the first light of dawn, a young Chinese girl found his body covered in a pool of vomit. He'd waited all night for his *Pops* to open up those beautiful red doors.

The Winner

When the winner was announced, it created a roar of cheers and applause from the audience, as the crowd slowly dispersed, many on their way down to the casino. Patrick accepted his money, and a small golden trophy, but he didn't remember any of it. Joshua came forward to make sure that he received everything he was due. Mara had finally managed to squeeze through the ropes, and held his head gently in her lap. He smiled up at her, touched her face, and his eyes slowly closed. She leaned forward and kissed his bloody mouth, pushing his wet bangs out of his eyes. Sarah was eventually able to find a doctor who saw to Patrick's injuries. They brought him home, wrapped in bandages. Jenjie and Joshua carried him up to his room and helped him to bed. Mara wouldn't leave his side. He ran a fever for the first few days and was delirious most of the time. Mrs. Levy asked her grandson to move in an extra cot so Mara could monitor him through the night and administer his medicines. She patiently washed his face, and tended to his injuries. His nose was badly broken, along with three cracked ribs, his kidneys swollen. His entire body was covered in cuts and bruises, and bound with bandages. She was careful to keep each one clean and fresh.

On Sunday morning, Jenjie dropped off a pot of fresh soup from the restaurant. His mother sent it along with a ceramic pot filled with antiseptic salve made from Chinese herbs. Mrs. Lee included some dried ginseng root inside a small glass jar. She left instructions with Jenjie, explaining how it could be made into tea to help speed the healing process. Mara and Sarah worked together preparing the salve and applying it gently to his wounds. Then they made several batches of ginseng tea. Mara tried her best to get Patrick to drink it. When he was somewhat awake, she'd spoon-fed him a bit of soup, until he fell back to sleep. In his delirium, he tossed and turned, sometimes crying out Mara's name. On the third day, his fever broke. It was early in the morning with the rain pounding against the bedroom window. Mara was looking over at him when his eyes opened.

His mouth pulled up in a lopsided grin. "Hello, little rose," he whispered hoarsely." She threw her arms around him, and he caressed the back of her hair—the rain kept falling.

* * * *

Mara helped Patrick downstairs for breakfast. He was famished, eating everything placed before him. His friends smiled in relief as he spooned up another helping of scrambled eggs. His face was covered in bruises, his right eye swollen, and his nose taped. Otherwise, he seemed ready for the world. After eating, he stood, and Mara rushed to his side. He smiled down at her patiently.

"Don't worry, darlin'. I'm going to be alright." He tried to assure her, but she noticed the pain in his eyes when he walked, and his broken ribs were still sore to the touch. He reached down and placed his arm around her waist as she led him toward the parlor. The rain pounded against the windowpanes, and Mrs. Levy tossed some wood in the fireplace. The housemates sat around, sipping hot chocolate.

Sarah turned toward Patrick. "It's such a relief that you're home safe. We've all been so worried about you, and we could barely get Mara to take a bite to eat while you've been recovering. She just couldn't bear to leave your side. I had her meals brought up to your room while you slept."

He looked up, reaching for her hand. "My little rose is quite the woman."

Her friends nodded in agreement.

A knock on the door made everyone turn. Mrs. Levy walked over to see who it was. A tall man, with steel gray eyes made his way into the room. He wore a faded brown duster and a Stetson hat. His dark hair was graying at the temples, and there were deep lines around his eyes. It was a handsome face, one that had seen all the good and the bad from San Francisco over the years.

"Sorry to barge in on you like this, but I have some interesting news." Patrick waved at him from his seat, and introduced the city's sheriff. Most had met him before, but it was Mara's first time. He smiled and took her hand.

"I've heard so much about you, Miss McClain. Patrick never gets tired of talking about you." She blushed, looking into his cool gray eyes. His crow's-feet deepening as he grinned.

"It's a pleasure to meet you, sir," Sarah took his hat and coat, and they made room for him on the couch. Miss Levy handed him a mug of fresh cocoa.

"Well, the last few days have been very revealing," he began. All eyes were on him as he went on. "On the night of Patrick's fight, I came down to talk to Mr. Williams. I'd planned to take him down for questioning after the crowds dwindled. I've been looking into his case after Patrick told me a little about his history in Ireland." Sheriff Carpenter folded his weather-beaten hands together, and quickly explained the rumors surrounding Katie and Daniel's murders. The friends looked at one another, dumbfounded.

"Well, I couldn't exactly go to Kinvara to investigate, so I decided to do a little background check on Mr. Williams right here in San Francisco, and it appears that he's been involved in a lot of dark dealings."

A murmur went around the room as he spoke. "Mr. Williams has apparently been mixed up in some shady gambling ventures in the city, mainly boxing and cards. He sponsored your opponent, Patrick. Samuel Johnson was his boy." Mr. Deane looked up, eyes widening. "And there's more. Samuel Johnson is dead."

They all gasped. "He was found outside of one of the opium dens in Chinatown after the fight. He'd overdosed. I was interested in talking to him on the account of the murder of a boxer a few years back. It's rumored that he killed one of his opponents in an alley, and some of the fighters mentioned that James Williams might have disposed of the body. This in itself would be enough to bring him in for questioning, but there's even more to the story," he said, shaking his head.

The group was silent as the sheriff detailed his investigation. "James Williams had been making quite a bit of money off of Samuel Johnson. He'd invested in several properties around the city. There have been quite a few complaints made against him for unfair renting practices. He's been known to threaten his clients, sometimes even physically. He'd often bring Samuel along as a kind of bodyguard. He'd kept them silent by intimidation. Only a handful of his tenants were willing to come forward and speak to me.

"His tactics proved profitable, and over the past few years he made a small fortune in real estate, but he became just a little too greedy. The rest that I'm about to explain is of a delicate nature, and I wouldn't like to disturb the ladies by it."

Sarah shook her head vehemently. "No, Sheriff, we're tough women, each one of us. There's not too much that can shock me after living in San Francisco all these years. Betty and Mara are definitely no shrinking violets, either. So, please go on."

The women all nodded in agreement.

Sheriff Carpenter studied Mrs. Levy's face. He nodded at her, a glimmer of fondness and respect in his eyes. "Very well, then." He looked at Patrick as he explained the rest of his story. "James Williams apparently was very fond of the opium dens in Chinatown. He was very partial to *The Red Doors*. He enjoyed spreading his money around. He was also a frequent guest at *Lola's Ladies*, the whorehouse on Kearny Street."

Mara's jaw tightened as she listened to this new information. He was certainly the vilest man she'd ever come across. The sheriff paused a moment before continuing, "Mr. Williams spent a small fortune on women and drugs. He also frequented several of the gambling houses in town, including a few of the back street Chinese game houses. The Tongs took notice when he became a regular. For those that aren't familiar with the Tongs, well, they're an organized gang of Chinese citizens involved in a lot of criminal activity, including making demands on their own people by charging protection fees—racketeering we call it. These men are in charge of most of Chinatown's drug dens, whorehouses, and gambling rooms.

"I spoke to several fighters, and they informed me that James Williams was expecting quite a payday from his boxer Samuel Johnson. He put a very large chunk of cash on the fight, probably figured he could pay off his gambling debts that way. Well, I don't think he ever imagined that he'd lose. He apparently fled right after the fight."

Mara took in a deep breath, a small glimmer of hope surfaced.

The sheriff went on to explain, "Several witnesses placed him at the Embarcadero shortly after the fight. He was spotted keeping company with a young woman. They boarded one of the ferries and haven't been seen since."

Mara's stomach tightened. She was certain that the young lady had to be Jane Darby. My God, the poor girl probably had no idea who she was dealing with. She said a silent prayer for her.

Joshua Cohen looked at the sheriff and said, "This must be why he's been withdrawing so much money from his accounts over the last few weeks."

Betty turned and asked, "What do you mean, Joshua?"

"Well, the bank tellers informed me just the other day that he'd been taking out significant withdrawals. We figured that he was getting ready to purchase another piece of property, and that he was paying in cash, but it sounds like he was using it to gamble. So, Mara, this really changes things for you."

"How is that?"

"He left his accounts very low this week. If he doesn't come back, and now that sounds quite unlikely, then your property can be picked back up by the bank. It would be available to either purchase or lease. As the bank manager, I'd give you first option," he grinned.

Betty kissed Joshua on the cheek. He flushed happily, and took her hand in his. Mara's eyes filled with tears as she thanked him. She then looked up at Patrick; he smiled; no words were needed. He'd gone to the sheriff like he'd promised, and now James Williams was hopefully miles away. The sheriff had uncovered a giant can of worms, all because Patrick had kept his word to keep her safe and protected.

"Sheriff, what does this mean for the investigation?"

"Ma'am, if this man comes anywhere near town, he'll be arrested. I'm going to send his information on to some neighboring cities, but as far as him coming back, well, I wouldn't hold my breath. I think your days dealing with James Williams are over."

The sheriff finished his last sip of cocoa and stood up. Mara rushed over and gave him a quick peck on the cheek. "Thank you so much. I can't even begin to tell you what this means. You've taken such a weight off me."

"It's my pleasure, ma'am. I'm happy to have helped." He walked over to Mrs. Levy and thanked her for the cocoa with an admiring smile. After he'd left, the friends talked over one another, barely able to contain their excitement. Donald stood up from his chair to make an announcement.

"This is such delightful news. I think we've all been through so much together these last few weeks. I think it's time we celebrate."

Jeremiah looked up with interest "That's a wonderful idea. What were you thinking?"

"The mayor visited the store yesterday. He invited us all to come join him at the Palace Hotel on Saturday. Everyone who is someone will be attending, and Mara, it would be a wonderful way for you to meet some new art patrons. There will be ballroom dancing, an orchestra, and delicious food and drinks." He spun around the floor, arms outstretched. He took Mara by the hand and guided her across the room. Their friends cheered them on.

"It sounds absolutely fabulous. The Palace Hotel is right down on Montgomery Street," Donald said, twirling Mara around in a graceful circle.

She looked toward Patrick, wondering if he'd be strong enough to go.

As if reading her mind, he slowly walked over, bowed, and reached for her hand. Donald smiled, gently releasing her into Patrick's arms. He swept her up, looking deep in her eyes, and gave her a quick peck on the nose.

"I think it's a wonderful idea, even if I'm limping a bit; I think it's the perfect way to celebrate."

Mara beamed up at him, thrilled that they would be going to their first dance together.

"Wonderful," Donald said, clapping his hands together, "We should all get dressed in our finest attire. Oh, yes, it's time to dust off our dancing shoes!"

The Gowns

The rain came down incessantly all week. Mara stayed by Patrick's side, helping him change his bandages, and assisting Sarah around the house. Their excitement grew as the day of the dance drew closer. On Thursday afternoon, Betty came back to the house early. She knocked softly on Mara's bedroom door. She entered and immediately began pacing back and forth. Mara watched her patiently, waiting for her to begin.

She smiled at Betty and asked, "Is something on your mind?"

Well…yes, it's just…I'm really excited for the dance on Saturday…but I'm feeling a little unprepared."

"Why is that?"

"You see," she hesitated, "it's just I don't' really have anything really suitable to wear, and this is going to be the first time Joshua and I go out dancing."

Mara was pensive for a moment, and then had an idea. "Why don't we go down to the mercantile store, Donald's always begging me to look at their dresses. Did you know that he actually made several of them by hand?"

"Oh?" Betty smiled eyes widening, but I wouldn't know where to start. Would you help me?"

"I'd love to…and actually, I'm overdue for a new gown myself." Mara looked out the window, noticing that the rain was letting up.

"Why don't we just go over now?"

"Oh, could we?" She asked, bursting with excitement. The women grabbed their coats and went arm and arm down the street, their faces flushed in the cool autumn air. Donald was sitting by the register reading a book. He looked up as they entered the store.

"Ladies, what a pleasure! What can I help you with today?"

"Mara looked at Betty who seemed at a loss for words. "We're here for your help, Donald. I know this is quite short notice, but we thought we might look at your dresses in the back?"

His eyes grew wide, and he sighed. "I'd thought you'd never ask." He offered them his arms and smiled. "Shall we, girls?"

"We shall," they giggled.

They made their way to the modest boutique and they looked at an array of dresses. Donald studied them for a moment before going to the back rack. "What you ladies need are gowns that will flatter your figures and bring out your lovely eyes. Oh, yes," he said to himself.

After a few minutes of searching, he chose two gowns. They took turns trying them on in the back dressing room. Betty slipped on a dark green satin dress, which Mara helped cinch tightly around her delicate waist. She'd gasped when her friend turned around. She'd never noticed her shapely curves before or her long legs. Her body was normally hidden under layers of calico and homespun cotton.

"Oh, Betty, you look so beautiful!"

They walked out of the changing room, and Donald studied her carefully. He walked around her slowly with his measuring tape. "This looks fabulous on you, dear. It just needs to be taken in about half an inch at the waist. And believe me, that's a wonderful problem to have," he chuckled. "But just look at you! Such a lovely figure," he sighed.

Then it was Mara's turn. He offered her a soft cornflower blue gown. It was crushed velvet, with a gold buttons and fringed lace. There was a small bustle in the back, and the ruffled layers cascaded down to the floor like ocean waves.

When she opened the door, her friends looked at each other speechless. Donald came forward, holding his breath. "Dear lord, if this wasn't the gown for you, then I can't imagine what would be. Just look at the way it brings out your blue eyes! And I do believe…yes…it's a perfect fit. I sewed these dresses myself. It's almost as if I had you ladies in mind when I made them. There's just a couple of more things you'll need," he said thoughtfully. He sorted through a collection of hair accessories until he found the perfect ones. He handed Mara a soft blue rose clip, and gave Betty a velvet green daisy. Then, he showed them several pairs of shoes, finding them perfect ones, which matched their dresses. They took their purchases to the counter, and paid at the register. Donald made sure to give them both a generous friends and family discount. He assured Betty that he'd have her dress altered by Saturday.

After saying their goodbyes, they headed back to the house. The rain had started up again, so they rushed home quickly. The next few days were cold and damp, storms followed by more storms. Patrick was now able to get around by himself, and Mara stayed in her own bedroom at night. She slipped off to sleep with the sounds of rain striking her bedroom window. That night, she dreamed of a beautiful parlor, golden leaves dancing in the air, and soft lights mirrored within stained glass windows. She murmured softly in her sleep, a smile moving over her face as she whispered the words, Autumn Lady.

The Palace Hotel

Mara and Betty busied themselves preparing for the dance. They took turns helping each other get ready, cinching and buttoning their layers of silk and velvet. Betty's hands shook as she worked her hair into a severe bun. Mara worried that if she stretched it any tighter her eyes would fall out of her head.

Betty turned with a look of frustration, tears welling. "I've never been good at fixing myself up, I guess. My pa helped me when I was a little girl, but he didn't know what he was doing," she sighed. "Any suggestions?"

Mara led her to the vanity and had her sit down on the velvet seat. She studied her for a moment before going to her collection of combs and brushes.

"May I?"

Betty nodded, a helpless look in her eyes. Mara busied herself undoing the taut bun. Soft waves fell down her back and shoulders. She stared in stunned disbelief.

"Your hair is absolutely gorgeous! I had no idea how long it was. It's always pulled back so proper."

A smile lit up her face as she turned her friend away from the mirror. She lifted a silver brush in the air and began combing through loose strands, the tawny highlights glistening in the fading light. They pooled around her shoulders like soft ocean waves. Satisfied, she studied her face with interest.

"I have a little powder and rouge if you'd like to try it?"

Betty nodded, a hint of excitement in her eyes, and then, to Mara's amazement, she reached for her glasses, folded them, and placed them on the vanity. Mara took a deep breath. It was the first time she'd ever seen Betty without them. Her eyes were like two emeralds, almost feline.

"Can you see without them?"

"Yes, I use them mostly for reading, but I'm always misplacing them, so I just keep them on all the time." She sighed.

Mara smiled. She sorted through her powder and rouge collection, selecting soft shades to compliment her friend's complexion. When she was finished, she turned Betty to face the mirror.

"Is that really me?" she gasped.

"Yes. And you're absolutely gorgeous!"

"Oh, Mara!" She stood, wrapping her arms around her best friend. The ladies finished with their hair accessories, and helped themselves to a crystal decanter, applying drops of floral perfume to their necks and wrists. They smiled at one another and made their way downstairs.

Joshua and Patrick were waiting on the sofa, corsages in hand. They looked up and their jaws dropped. They stood as the women entered. Joshua walked over to Betty, reaching for her hair. His hand grazed the soft waves, the strands falling between his fingers. She smiled as his eyes traveled over her face, gazing into her emerald eyes. He suddenly found himself leaning in for a kiss. His mouth brushed her lips, as he traced his fingers across her cheek.

Mara smiled at Patrick. He reached for her hands, his dark eyes smoldering in the fading light. "You're the most beautiful woman I've ever laid eyes on," he whispered. He looked at the corsage he was holding, delicate violets with small white roses.

"May I?"

Mara nodded happily. He reached down, taking her hand, and gently placed the flowers around her wrist. Donald opened the door to let the women pass, eyeing their dresses with satisfaction. Mara looked up and whispered, "Thank you." He smiled softly and nodded.

Patrick and Joshua escorted their dates outside. Sarah Levy and Sheriff Carpenter followed close behind. The sheriff had been coming by the house quite a bit since his Sunday visit. He'd eventually summed up the courage to ask Sarah to accompany him to the dance. She'd accepted the invitation with pleasure. Donald and Jeremiah followed, closing the door behind them. They took separate carriages, a cool breeze following them into the fading light.

The Palace Hotel was a beautiful building—a spacious ballroom with overhanging chandeliers, dramatic marble statues and an impressive art collection. Landscape scenes filled the opaque walls. A skylight opened to reveal a blanket of stars. They appeared to dance across the inky darkness, a harvest moon lighting their way. An orchestra played in the background—a collection of cellos, violins, and wind instruments were on display. The musicians wore identical black suits, their faces masked in concentration as they synchronized with perfect harmony.

Mrs. Levy and her housemates mingled for the first hour, enjoying appetizers and glasses of champagne. Mara and Betty admired the well-dressed ladies showing off the latest fashions from Europe, cascading layers of satin held up by bustles and underskirts. The women glided through the crowds, their pleated gowns rustling softly with every step. Corsets bound in whalebone and leather cinched many of the women tightly. Their layers restrained them in breathless rigidity.

The latest hairstyles demanded dramatic curls, bangs that swept over the forehead, capped with dainty bonnets. Wigs were common, as extensions were added to one's natural hair. Many of the ladies wore velvet collars around their necks, the latest fashion trend out of Europe. They chatted among themselves, their gentle laughter ringing out like little bells, fanning themselves, as they mingled.

The mayor made his way over to Mara and her friends. A middle-age woman with a snowy puff of white hair followed him. She looked intently at the group, taking them in with an appraising air. She held their gazes, shaking hands firmly as they were introduced. Mayor Selby offered warm greetings and introduced them to Elizabeth Cady Stanton. He made sure to express his admiration for his friend, explaining how she was a leader in The Women's Suffrage Movement, and actively seeking a woman's right to vote. She took Mara aside to speak to her privately.

"It's a pleasure to meet you, Miss McClain. I was so excited to hear how a young woman had successfully opened a gallery in town. I imagine it's been quite challenging in this male dominated city," she said, her mouth pulling down in a grimace.

Mara smiled, meeting her direct gaze. "It's been quite the adventure, but both men and women have helped me along the way. So, I count myself lucky."

Mrs. Stanton put her hands together. "I've been traveling quite a bit this past year, often with my friend Susan B. Anthony. We've been trying to spread the word…to plant seeds of change in the minds of those that seek justice. We want a future that will allow women the opportunity to vote. For far too long our voices have been silenced, our ideas disregarded. I hope you'll join us in making this happen."

A glimmer of interest surfaced in her eyes. "I'd be happy to hear more about your movement. It's about time we were allowed the legal right to voice our opinion in politics."

The older woman nodded in agreement. She was quite taken with Mara and wanted her to be caught up on all of the latest news regarding the suffrage movement. She explained how she'd been an active member of the abolitionists as well. She was very proud of her involvement, and more than happy to see the end of slavery, but things changed dramatically after the Emancipation Proclamation. Many of the group's leaders had lost interest in the fight for women's rights. Mara listened in fascination. Mrs. Stanton was a force to be reckoned with, a tornado of energy and passion. She was impressed by her sharp intellect, her approach being at once both engaging and commanding. Her eyes would darken, when she spoke of the oppression of women, and then shine passionately as she explained the goals of the suffrage movement. She wanted a world where women could speak freely about their opinions, even to hold office in the political arena. She handed Mara a pamphlet detailing the movement. After a lengthy discussion, Mrs. Stanton said her goodbyes and began making her way around the room, preaching her dreams of equality and a better tomorrow.

There were many people that sought out Mara's audience that evening, a good number of which showed an interest in her gallery. Others simply admired her attractive features and graceful charms. As such, she was embraced by San Francisco's high society and its many elite members, politicians and businessmen alike. Many fashionably dressed women expressed an appreciation for her gown. Mara always directed them back over to Donald, explaining his talents. He soon had a crowd of ladies fussing over him. He engaged all of them with a dramatic flair and exuberance. His admirers flocked around, inquiring if he might design some of their dresses. He assured them that he could definitely help with their fashion needs, inviting them to visit his boutique. They accepted happily, and he continued keeping court with his entourage.

Patrick was also approached during the evening. Many wanted to congratulate him on winning the fight, and they were all curious about his future plans. Several women stole glances his way, admiring his handsome features and remarking on his many bruises. His injuries only made him appear more exotic and dangerous—a winning combination for those who sought an escape from the constraints of privilege.

He met a few businessmen that were curious about his interest in real estate, and the desire to build new homes in Pacific Heights. One man, Steven Jacobson, had earned quite a bit of money betting on Patrick's fight. He explained that he would enjoy speaking to him further regarding his new business venture. They shook hands and planned to meet up later in the week.

In the corner of the room stood a man in black. His eyes followed Patrick as he mingled. He wrung his hands absently, making his way over to the group of men discussing the fight. He listened, but did not contribute. The other men appeared not to notice, just one more well-to-do businessman interested in boxing. The gentleman took turns congratulating Patrick, except for the pale stranger. He simply stared, a slight tremor flickering over his right eye. He wiped at it absently, slowly backing away from the crowd, and then he was gone.

Mara and Patrick eventually found one another. The orchestra was playing the Blue Danube waltz and dancers were making their way out to the ballroom floor. The couples spun around in graceful circles, keeping in time with the music. Patrick escorted Mara into the sea of silk and lace. He took her in his arms, gracefully leading her around the marble floor. She took a deep breath, amazed by his skillful dancing. She noticed that he occasionally grimaced, not completely healed, though he smiled, doing his best to please her.

Joshua and Betty soon joined them. They gazed intently into one another's eyes, lost and in love. Then, Sheriff Carpenter and Sarah Levy joined the crowd. They twirled about the ballroom, under the vast stars shining above the skylight. Donald and Jeremiah were helping themselves to crystal flutes of champagne, nodding happily as they watched them dance.

Patrick was light on his feet, guiding Mara across the dance floor, her periwinkle dress cascading around her like sails on the ocean. As the music drew to an end, Patrick kissed her cheek, lowering himself gingerly to the floor. When he reached for her hand, her eyes widened, and the entire room fell silent.

"Mara, you're truly my heart and soul. I can't imagine my life without you, and I feel so very blessed that I've found you. You're the most amazing woman—passionate, loving, and so breathtakingly gorgeous. I live for your smile…your lovely blue eyes. I want to give you a beautiful life, one full of magic and my devotion. I love yah, little rose.

"So, Miss Mara Elizabeth McClain, would you do me the honor of being my wife?" He held out a velvet box; inside was a rosette diamond ring, surrounded by crystal blue sapphires. The brilliant gems sparkled under the evening sky. Mara took a deep breath, looking down with tears in her eyes. Her lips parted, and she cried, "Oh yes, Mr. Deane, yes!"

Patrick placed the ring on her finger, swept her up in his arms, kissing her softly in the candlelight. The room exploded with applause. Their friends rushed over to congratulate them, offering up hugs and kisses. The night was truly magical, one they would look back on for years to come, dreaming of the night they twirled beneath the stars.

Donald Becker

The morning of their wedding was bright with sunshine. Betty and Sarah busied themselves getting the bride ready. The gown was white silk with cascading layers and embroidered roses throughout. The day after their engagement announcement, Donald had invited Mara to the store. He took her by the hand and brought her upstairs to show off his new art studio and sewing room. He seemed a little nervous, his eyes darting around the room. Mara reached for his arm and asked, "Is everything all right?"

He looked into her eyes, exhaling. "I wanted to give you a wedding present, if you're interested," he said, wringing his hands and fidgeting. "Would you consider…perhaps having your dress designed by me," he whispered.

Mara's eyes flashed with excitement as she took his hand in hers, squeezing tightly.

"Oh, Donald, yes. It'd be an honor!"

He hugged her and grinned. "I was hoping you would say that!"

He led her to the back of the room and showed her the patterns he'd been considering. She studied them, noting the various styles and materials. Together, they chose a design, which would be form fitting at the bodice with a bib of needle lace cinched tightly around the waist, allowing for cascading layers. A long train of satin would be beaded with rows of delicate white roses. Donald was quiet as Mara explained her vision of the perfect wedding dress. His eyes glimmered with purpose while he took note of every detail.

* * * *

He worked on the gown incessantly all the way up to the day of the wedding, putting his heart and soul into every stitch. When he presented it to her and her eyes immediately filled with tears. She kissed his cheek, and he blushed and looked down at the floor. Betty and Sarah held their breath as they studied the beautiful craftsmanship. It was a dress suitable for a princess. They followed her into her bedroom and went to work helping her get ready. Mara's hands were shaking as the hour drew closer. When they'd finished, she turned to the window and looked out onto the street. Almost time for church. She exhaled and walked toward the vanity, to look at her reflection. Her friends stood by her side. Sarah went to the back of the room, retrieving a long lace veil.

"Mara, you're like my own daughter. I'd like to present this veil to you as something borrowed," she said.

Mara admired the lacy material, delicate and refined. Her blue eyes filled with tears as it was placed on her head.

"Don't you dare cry, Mara. You'll get me started and I'll be doing plenty of that at the church."

Betty came forward with a small box in her hand. "Mara, you're my best friend…actually more like my sister. I know you should have something blue, and so I want you to wear my mother's necklace on your special day. My pa gave it to me on my sixteenth birthday. It was a gift to my mother on their anniversary," she whispered.

She turned, her mouth trembling. "Oh, Betty, it's so beautiful." She looked down at the sapphire, admiring the brilliant gem. "I'll take good care of it for you." She hugged her tightly, kissing her cheek.

"I can't thank you enough, and to think you're going to be my Maiden and Matron of honor!" They wrapped their arms around their friend and led her outside to the surrey, carefully placing her train alongside her on the seat. Betty rode with Joshua, while Sarah drove Mara. Autumn leaves blew across the cobblestones, colorful markers of time.

The Wedding

Patrick and Jenjie took a detour on the way to the wedding. They'd made an early start of the day. The groom had planned a special surprise for his bride. There were many people out on the road that morning, and neither man realized that they were being followed. They parked in the alley behind a large warehouse. Jenjie busied himself tying Sammy to a hitching post while Patrick searched for his toolbox in the back of the wagon. He was oblivious to the approaching footsteps. A shadow fell over him and he turned towards the darkness. A stranger was blocking the light, a shiny pistol in hand. The man appeared to be in his thirties, well dressed, but disheveled. The right side of his cheek appeared swollen.

"Put your hands out where I can see them," he said with a gravelly voice.

"Who are you?"

"That's not important. All you need to know is that you cost me everything."

Patrick looked up in question, his brows knitting together, "I think there's been some kind of mistake…I've never seen you before."

The stranger pointed the gun at Patrick's head, smiling wildly. "James assured me that you were going to lose. He said it was a sure thing. I bet everything I had on the fight. You…shouldn't even be here," he growled.

"I won the fight fairly. I'm sure we can talk about this reasonably…if you just put the gun away. Shooting me isn't going to fix your problem."

The stranger's face reddened, his eyes narrowed. "No, but I'm sure that you won a pretty penny. You're not even from this country, are you?" He tongue darted over his bottom lip. "You don't deserve the money." He spit a clump of tobacco towards Patrick's feet. A trail of brown spittle ran down his chin, over his rust-colored beard. "So, you're going to hand it over to me…and then…maybe I'll consider letting you go."

Patrick studied the man's face. He noticed the beads of sweat on his forehead and upper lip. A nervous twitch flickering over his right eye.

"I…don't have the cash on me."

"Then we can go for a little ride. My carriage is parked out back. Move," he said, gesturing with his pistol.

Jenjie quietly crept up behind the man. He tossed a pebble towards his feet. The moment the stranger's attention was diverted, he hurled himself forward. He dropped his gun, but not before pulling the trigger, the bullet whizzing within inches of Patrick's face. The loud re-percussion exploded like thunder. Jenjie wrapped his arm around the assailant's throat in a chokehold, dropping him to his knees. He gasped for breath, struggling on the ground. Patrick rushed over, his eyes wide. "Thank you, Jenjie," he said with a sigh of relief.

A second man appeared in the alley and hurried over.

"Wow! You two definitely keep things interesting around here." He looked back and forth between the men shaking his head. "I was just checking on your order inside, Mr. Deane. They're ready for you." He put his hands on his hips, looking down the alley. "Look, why don't you head on over. Maybe Mr. Lee can help me secure this man inside my carriage while you get set up. I can't wait to hear what this is all about," he said. He studied the man on the ground struggling to get up. Jenjie pushed his knee into the small of his back and the stranger groaned in protest. "I suppose that I could take him to the sheriff's office. I believe you two have a wedding to make?"

"Yes, we most definitely do. I really appreciate your help."

"My pleasure. I won a lot of money off your fight. Like I was saying at the dance, I'm looking forward to going into business with you fellows. I hope you enjoy your wedding gift…as a little advance on our upcoming business." He handed Patrick a gold key on a chain.

"Thank you, Mr. Jacobson. We'll definitely enjoy it."

"Wonderful. I'm looking forward to getting to work once you're back in town. Mr. Lee and I can start looking at properties while you're away.

"Sounds great. I'll get in touch after we get back from the honeymoon. Thanks again."

Jenjie and Patrick took care of their final errand before the wedding, and then rushed back to the church with just a few moments to spare.

* * * *

Mara and her friends arrived at Saint Patrick's; a large number of carriages were already parked outside. They waited in the back, nervously anticipating the ceremony. The procession lined up, with Father Joseph following behind. When the music began, the congregation rose to their feet. All eyes turned toward Mara. She appeared to float down through the aisle, an angel decked out in all white. Her bouquet of pink roses matched the glow of her blushing cheeks. Tears and sighs greeted her as she passed. Donald led her by the arm, smiling proudly. Joshua escorted Betty, followed by Mrs. Levy on Sheriff Carpenter's arm.

The groom stood tall and proud in a dark navy suit, a silk vest over a white silken shirt. A few loose bangs escaped over his forehead. His brown eyes glistened with tears as Mara made her way down the aisle. Jenjie stood next to him as best man. He smiled softly, honored to be part of his friend's special day. Patrick took a deep breath, overcome with emotion. Donald led the bride to the altar, stepping forward when the priest inquired as to who was giving her away. He gave her a quick peck on the cheek and made his way back down the aisle, taking a seat next to Jeremiah. Mr. Smith noticed the tears in his eyes and gently patted his shoulder.

Sarah's grandson handed Patrick the ring when the time came. He slipped it carefully on her finger as they said their vows. A feeling of peace washed over them while they gazed into one another's eyes, enraptured by love and grace. Applause rang out when they took their first kiss as husband and wife. Afterwards, the couple made their way down the aisle as Mr. And Mrs. Deane. The congregation rose to their feet, their friends' good wishes and showers of rice followed them.

Outside, the weather had taken a startling turn. The sky was darkening, and a storm front was moving in. Patrick leaned toward Mara and whispered, "I have a little surprise for you, love."

She looked up at her husband, her heart filled with wonder. At the bottom of the steps was a new carriage—navy blue, with gold accents. A large satin bow was tied around the back. She smiled when she saw that Sammy was hitched to the front, but when he leaned down, she noticed that another horse was standing alongside him. Patrick took her hand and led her to the other side. A petite, sorrel mare whinnied as they approached. Mara's eyes widened with disbelief, her mouth falling open.

Patrick smiled, pushing his bangs away with the back of his hand. "It's about time we had our own carriage, and I know how much you love horses. So, I figured you might enjoy one of your very own, and this little mare was just released from the SPCA for adoption. She needed a new home, and so I thought it'd be nice for her to join our family."

"Oh, Patrick, it's the pony from that terrible accident, but look at her now! Why she's filled out so...you can't even see her ribs. She's so beautiful. I...love her."

He smiled and nodded. "They took good care of her at the shelter."

Mara reached up and stroked her neck. The mare eyed her softly and snorted. Sammy nudged her as they leaned close.

"Looks like Sammy's quite taken with her."

"Like I told you when we first met, love...Sammy can't resist a pretty lady." He offered his arm and helped her into the carriage. Mara sighed as she sat down on the velvet cushions, feeling like a princess. Their friends waved goodbye as they made their way down the cobblestone road.

The Honeymoon

They traveled for many miles along the glistening bay, past forested valleys and meadows of ice plant. A few hours into the journey, the clouds gathered and the wind began to moan. Patrick pulled Mara close, rubbing her arms to warm her. She was filled with an excited anticipation, wondering where they were going. As the afternoon light faded, a sea breeze blew against their faces and the crashing tides echoed from the shore. A light drizzle fell, and they blinked away the cold drops. They eventually arrived at a small fishing village. Clusters of willows were strewn throughout sandy beaches. A foghorn sounded from the distance. It was answered by a series of barks from a group of shiny sea lions. They huddled in lazy contentment, yawning and stretching in their protected cove. A sliver of sunlight escaped the cloud barrier, warming their plump bodies.

There were anchored ships in the distance, hulking giants. A scattering of smaller boats floated along the restless waves, tiny dots on an infinite sea. Several rustic cottages were strewn along the beach. Mara wondered if they would be safe with the rising tides. The full moon was helping draw the waters dangerously close to the shore.

They drove past an old faded sign reading, The Village of Sausalito. It was a sleepy town full of seasoned mariners with weather-beaten faces and calloused hands. The shoreline was dotted with modest shops and cafés. Shacks lined the road, providing local fisherman with bait and tackle. The carriage weaved along the dirt path, passing churning waters and rocky dunes. The azure tides rushed and crashed, seagulls occasionally diving toward the waters, their shrill voices crying in the wind.

Patrick looked at his bride, his eyes shining with love and eagerness. The road curved toward a sandy beach, which was surrounded by steep rock cliffs. A modest cottage was set between the tall boulders, providing its own private setting. Mara wondered why the home was set apart from the others. A small paddock rested behind the house. He pulled their carriage toward the stalls, parked, and helped Mara down from her seat. Her shoes slipped into the sandy soil, and so he steadied her as they walked.

She looked up questioning Patrick, her eyebrows rising.

"You like it, love?"

"Oh, it's a beautiful town. So charming, but why are we here?"

"Darlin', I wanted us to enjoy a nice little vacation for our honeymoon, and I thought this fishing village might be a private place to…begin our lives together," he said, with his eyes glimmering in the fading light.

"I've been working with a gentleman I met at the Palace Hotel. You remember Mr. Jacobson? We chatted briefly at the dance. He's involved in quite a few real-estate ventures in the city. He also won a large amount of money on my fight. Boxing happens to be his favorite sport. So, he's interested in doing some business with Jenjie and me. We're planning on investing together in the Pacific Heights neighborhood. This cottage happens to be one of his vacation properties. He offered it to us for our honeymoon," he said.

Her mouth fell open when she realized what he'd planned. "Oh, Patrick, this is so beautiful!" She wrapped her arms around him, as he leaned down for a kiss.

He smiled softly, and then tended to their horses, setting them up next to one another in their own stalls. Each was given a flake of hay and some scoops of grain. They leaned toward their feed, blowing vapors of mist in the chilly air. Mara studied the sorrel mare, admiring her glossy coat and petite frame. The setting sun slipped through the window, blanketing them with its garnet glow. She reached her hand over the paddock door and stroked the white stripe running down the mare's muzzle. She nibbled at her fingers playfully, her velvet nose soft to the touch.

"She's so lovely, Patrick."

"Have you thought of a name yet, darlin?"

She tilted her head slightly. "I think that I'm going to call her Calliope. That's the Greek muse of poetry. It's fitting. She's so graceful when she trots, her dainty feet seem to dance along the ground. She's poetry in motion."

Patrick shook his head and smiled, "That's a beautiful name, and I was thinking we might want to take them down to the beach later this week. We could ride them along the shore together. Calliope is the perfect size for your tiny frame," he said, offering his arm. Mara nodded happily, imagining their horses racing together in the sand.

They made their way down a curving path, leading to the weatherworn cottage. Their feet sunk into the sand as they walked, leaving soft footprints behind. The sea breeze was fresh, the sky above glowing with crimson streaks. A harvest moon illuminated the waves in its hazy glow. They crashed together in frenzied harmony, the tide rising out to meet them. A crack of thunder erupted overhead, and the rain began to fall. A sprinkle at first, followed by icy sheets. They laughed, running towards the cottage hand in hand. Patrick unlatched the white picket fence, and they followed the graveled walkway to the oak door.

Mara looked around the front yard. Bright pink roses shot up toward the heavens, an ivory fountain resting between them. The rain caressed the snowy angel wings. The cherub grinned under the fading light. Patrick searched inside his pockets until he found the key, placing it inside the rusty lock. It jiggled for a moment before clicking open. He pushed on the door creaking on rusty hinges. He paused and looked down into Mara's soft blue eyes. He took her in his arms, the waves of silk fluttering in the breeze. They crossed the threshold, and he gently lowered her to the floor. The room was filled with shadows, a fading twilight outside the windows. A fireplace rested in the corner of the room. The mantel above displayed pieces of driftwood, a tiny ship in a bottle, and pink and white seashells. A large canvas hung above it—an ocean scene with raging tides and a moonlit sky. A bed sat opposite, covered in a navy and white quilt, a wedding ring pattern appliquéd to the soft cotton.

Patrick took Mara's hand, kissing it softly, and told her he'd be right back. He bent down in front of the fireplace and went to work starting the flames. Soon, the shadows disappeared into the corners and the hearth burned brightly. Mara studied his silhouette. Each movement highlighted the contours of his muscles along his back and arms. Outside the wind howled, a crash of thunder erupting followed by a streak of lightning that lit up the room. Mara jumped when it struck, letting out a gasp of surprise. Patrick turned toward her. The firelight reflecting in his dark eyes, golden highlights mirrored in the flames. His lips parted as he sighed. "I've never seen anyone so lovely, Mrs. Deane."

Hearing her new name made her heart flutter. He stepped closer, studying her face. Another roar of thunder rumbled, and the rain pounded against the doors and windows. Outside, the waves crashed like battling titans. He swept her up in his arms, his chiseled body pressing close. He carried her to the bed, his eyes dark as night. He leaned forward, kissing her mouth, and she responded eagerly. His hands moved over satin curves, loosening fasteners and ties. Mara freed his buttons, one by one, exposing his broad chest. She traced her fingers over taut muscles, exhaling in anticipation. She breathed in the scent of his aftershave and sun dried leather. He looked down at her delicate camisole and smiled. His hands moved across her shoulders, barely touching her skin, and the straps slid down. Undergarments fell to the ground, and his trousers soon followed.

Her eyes widened in the firelight. He reached his hand under the small of her back, carefully lowering her down toward the bed.

In that moment, Mara's heart pounded so hard she thought it might actually explode. Patrick caressed her body, sending tingling sensations down into her toes. She felt the gold of her wedding band, a reminder that she was now his wife, bound by the eternal. As their bodies pressed against one another, she trembled with anticipation, Patrick gazing into her soft blue eyes, tracing the curves of her face with the back of his hand.

"I love you, Mrs. Deane. I want you to know that you will always be my beautiful little rose. I pray that I'll be able to make you happy, and that you realize just how much I love yah, and I'll spend the rest of my life trying to make your dreams come true."

"I love you, Mr. Deane," she whispered, "and you've already made all of my dreams come true."

His dark eyes glowed like burning coals, his smile flashing brilliantly in the firelight. He pulled her closer, his hands caressing her strawberry blonde curls, their colorful strands slipping through his fingers, as her golden highlights shimmered in the night. His lips brushed over her mouth and down her delicate neck. His tongue flicked over her supple breasts. She pulled his face closer, her fingers clutching his wavy locks. He was eager to please, and her body yearned for his touch. He took his time until she couldn't take it anymore, and then she pressed against him, her body trembling, waiting for the secret to be revealed. He looked into her eyes making sure she was ready, and then pressed down gently with his hips.

When he entered, she winced slightly, biting down on her lower lip. He hesitated, her eyes widening with concern. She sighed and whispered, "Yes." The corners of his mouth pulled up, and he continued. The rain pounded on the roof and windows. A howling wind whipped against the cottage walls. Inside they were warm and safe in each other's arms. The firelight reflected in her locks of cinnamon gold. He smiled down in fascination, never knowing such happiness. Patrick's eyes were so full of love that Mara felt like she was falling.

His hands reached back, easing her hips closer. Their eyes locked and lips parted. When they joined together, their souls merged into one. They were no longer connected to the earth. They moved across sea and storm, and the universe rejoiced.

For the next week, they spent their days walking along the beach, hand in hand, exploring the town of Sausalito. They took their meals by candlelight and danced under a blanket of stars. At sunset, they would climb on their horses and ride along the shore, the ocean spray mirroring the moonlight, and then they would rush back to their little cottage, to make love until dawn's first light. Their eyes would never tire of one another. When they were old and gray, their children with little ones of their own, they would hold one another by the firelight and Patrick would whisper words of love to his little Irish rose.

Autumn Lady

October 1st, 1873 was a bright autumn day in the city of San Francisco. Mara stood in the front of a grand estate, her horse Calliope peacefully by her side. Jenjie smiled and set down his brush. "I'm finished with the painting if you'd like to take a look."

Her eyes widened as she hurried over to the canvas. She studied the striking brushstrokes, the brilliant ocean blue hue of her dress and bonnet. Mara's strawberry blonde curls shimmered like gold dust. Calliope's sorrel coat sparkled in the soft light. An electric current flowed over the figures. The dabs of paint had captured a specific and special moment in time.

She took Jenjie's hand and gave him a quick peck on the cheek. It's absolutely gorgeous. I'm going to have it hung in the parlor where everyone can see.

He grinned, busying himself by putting away the paints. Behind them, sheltered by the shade of a great oak, old friends enjoyed an outdoor picnic. The chilly wind scattered autumn leaves over the checkered tablecloth. Betty and Joshua watched their little boy chasing his shadow across the grass. Isaac Cohen stood with his mop of golden curls and his mother's vivid green eyes. Donald offered a bowl of salad to Jeremiah. Mrs. Levy passed a platter of potato latkes down to Sheriff Carpenter. He smiled, helping himself to a generous portion. Mara noticed they were running low on iced tea, and so she grabbed the pitcher and made her way back to the house.

She believed they would be toasting one another after they heard her news. She opened the double doors and headed into the parlor.

Autumn light shimmered through the stained glass windows, dancing crystals flickering across the walls. She studied the beams with fascination. She still couldn't believe that her husband created this beautiful home with his own two hands. It was breathtaking. The warm rays of the sun fell against her skin, settling on her growing waist. She looked down at her belly, a feeling of love so powerful that it nearly swept her away. Her hand reached down, caressing the modest bump, and for a brief moment she thought she could hear its heartbeat. Patrick walked behind her, gently placing his hand around her waist. He kissed her cheek, entwining his finger in hers. She turned toward him, his dark eyes full of love. "Are you feeling alright?"

"Yes," she said, "I was just going in for some more iced tea."

"Oh, you really need to rest, darlin'," he said, his brows knitting together. You're in a delicate state." He traced his fingers over her cheek, his eyes widening.

She laughed and shook her head, her curls bouncing around her shoulders, "I'm fine, love."

He smiled down at her and gave her a kiss on the nose. "I'm sure you are, but let me help you anyway."

He took her arm, escorting her to the back kitchen, and then helped carry the pitcher over to their friends. Mara and Patrick made sure everyone had a glass in hand. Just as he was preparing to speak, a loud clanging sounded from down the hill. Laughter floated on the wind as a blue and white cable car made its way past. Several passengers waved from the open windows as they traveled up the steep road.

Isaac's plump legs raced across the lawn, stopping inches from the wrought iron fence. He reached his chubby fingers through the bars, pointing towards the speeding trolley, teetering on overhanging cables. He jumped up and down, shouting and clapping, "Kaybee car!"

The friends giggled while Joshua lifted his son up onto his shoulder to get a better view, their golden curls highlighted by the autumn light. Patrick put his arm around Mara's waist, raising his glass in the air. All eyes were on them, anticipating a toast.

"We're so happy to have you all here to celebrate our house warming. Each and every one of you has been such a blessing in our lives. And we're hoping that as our family, you'll join us in celebrating some very exciting news." Their friends looked at each other, eyes widening. He took a deep breath, and his voice choked as he continued, "My little rose is expecting."

There were gasps and applause. Betty rushed over and hugged Mara, kissing her on the cheek. Donald followed behind, reaching for her hands.

"Oh, my goodness, I can't wait to get started on your little one's wardrobe. I have some patterns that would be absolutely perfect. I just need to find out if it's a boy or a girl…well maybe I'll make both, and so we'll be ready for the next one as well," he said hugging her close.

Mara kissed his cheek, her eyes glistening with tears, "You're a dream come true, Donald."

The friends took turns toasting. Afterwards, they helped clear the table and went back inside to sit by the fireplace. Jenjie helped Patrick hang the new painting on the parlor wall. Mara looked up at the portrait, her mouth trembling. She shook her head back and forth, her hand against her heart.

"Oh, it's absolutely stunning, Jenjie. I can't even tell you what this means to me." She reached her arms up and he smiled, hugging her gently against his chest.

Isaac ran over, pointing with outstretched hands. "Look at the beautiful autumn lady!"

Her friends looked toward the painting, flickers of golden light dancing along their silhouettes. Mara's tears trickled down her cheeks as she gazed in wonder. Patrick kissed her softly and whispered, "Yes, my autumn lady is very beautiful, indeed."

The Legacy

Mary closed the diary, the morning light flickering through the windowpane. When she stood, her legs tingled from sitting too long. Her mind raced, and her heart was beating with anticipation. She went back to her bedroom, quickly changed, and headed outside. Everything seemed clearer this morning, such a contrast from the day before. She noticed the sparkling dew on the pink rose bushes, their fragrant blossoms fresh in the morning sun. She'd planned to go back to her apartment this morning, but now everything had changed. She brought her Vespa down the cobblestone path, and let herself through the wrought iron fence.

The air was crisp and smelled faintly of chimney smoke. She traveled down Van Ness Avenue, heading to the Embarcadero. She parked her bike in front of the large procession of tents and food vendors. The city's farmers' market had drawn a large crowd this morning. People mulled around the various produce stands and craft tents. The aroma of fresh food mingled with the scent of herbs and spices. She walked past rows of tents, the soft morning light shining on the fall vegetables. A variety of orange and white pumpkins were displayed next to buckets of golden chrysanthemums. Yellow peppers appeared like shiny orbs in the soft morning light. She found her way to her favorite organic produce stand. A woman with dark red curls was busy helping a customer choose some heirloom tomatoes. She looked up and a smile spread over her face, "Mary, it's great to see you this morning. You're up early!"

She smiled at her friend, realizing that this was probably the last time she'd see her at the Embarcadero. "Katie, is this your last market?"

She nodded, pushing her curls out of her eyes with the back of her hand. "Yes, I'm moving next Saturday. It's been so crazy these past few weeks," she said, looking towards the bay. "But…I really need a change of scenery," she said.

Mary studied her face; it was a pretty one, but tired, dark circles under her eyes, streaks of gray highlighting her auburn hair. She'd been through a lot in the past year with her recent divorce. So, now she was getting ready to start all over in a brand new town, leaving everything she knew behind. Mary looked into her vivid green eyes. She noticed a little flicker of excitement that had been absent the past year. She hoped that her friend would find what she was looking for, perhaps some peace and solitude.

"Give me a call, if you're ever near Napa. You can stay in my cabin. There's a lake behind the house, a few acres of hiking and running trails. The country life is pretty peaceful, and I'll be starting a new market next spring. I have over fifteen acres to plant. It's exciting…but I know there's a lot of work ahead," she said.

Mary nodded and smiled, "I admire you, Katie. You know what you want and go for it. Good for you. I just inherited my grandmother's estate. There are a few bedrooms upstairs, so there's always room if you want to visit the city. I'm expecting some big changes myself. I think I finally found out what I want to do when I grow up." She laughed. "Well," she paused, "I guess I always knew; I was just a little too afraid to try."

Katie nodded, looking into her dark brown eyes, golden highlights flickering around the pupils. They had an unspoken understanding. They were both dreamers. Katie O'Brien was not only a farmer and businesswoman, but also an accomplished artist herself. They promised to keep in touch and exchanged addresses on their phones before leaving. The women hugged one another tightly. After saying goodbye, Mary made her way around the market, picking up a few fruits and vegetables, along with three breakfast sandwiches and headed back to the estate.

When she went inside, she noticed Margaret was busying herself in the kitchen, the aroma of fresh coffee in the air.

"Hello, Mary. I thought you were heading back to your apartment this morning. Everything all right?"

"Actually…I've had a change of plans. I'm going to be working in the studio today, and I picked up some breakfast sandwiches for us…so, don't worry about cooking. I just might need a little coffee."

Margaret studied her face, looking deep into her eyes. "I think coming back this morning was a wonderful idea. You look…peaceful. I'll be downstairs if you need anything, dear. And thank you for picking up breakfast."

She helped herself to a thermos of coffee and made her way upstairs. The storm clouds were gathering, and the rain trickled against the windows. She pulled back the studio curtains, revealing the gray cityscape. Mary stood in front of the unfinished canvas, studying soft blue eyes, which she knew held a secret.

A warm breeze blew against her face, the clanging of crystals echoing from the parlor. Her hand reached for the brush, hesitating for just a moment. She bit down on her lower lip and sighed. A dab of color hovered in the air until she released it. The dot joined perfectly with the others. She was pulled toward the light, and she was told a story. The canvas was a mirror, and the reflection was hers. The torch had been passed, and she knew that as long as they walked beside her, she'd never be alone. A smile spread over her face as she felt the spirit of many hands guiding her.

Outside the rain came down like blissful tears from heaven. She exhaled and whispered, "Autumn Lady."

ABOUT THE AUTHOR

AnneMarie Dapp

AnneMarie Dapp is a graduate of San Francisco State University, where she studied Studio Arts and Art History. She lives and writes on *Sock Monkey Ranch*, her and her husband Dale's vegetarian farm, in Prunedale, California.

For your reading pleasure, we invite you to visit our web bookstore

TORRID BOOKS

www.torridbooks.com